ACCLAIM FOR KEVIN BROCKMEIER'S

Things That Fall from the Sky

"Unique and spellbinding . . . Brockmeier is up to something different." —*Minneapolis Star Tribune*

"Lyrical. . . . Brockmeier is clearly a talent. The stories are filled with the kinds of metaphors that make you see the world afresh." —*Shout*

"There is magic at work here. Brockmeier combines a fearless, fantastic imagination with a warm heart, and the resulting stories are brimming with mystery, sadness, and moments of exquisite beauty."
—Judy Budnitz, author of *If I Told You Once*

"Brockmeier . . . achieves melancholy brilliance. . . . *Things That Fall* is perfect for reading at bedtime, when the mind is most likely to accept Brockmeier's invitations to strange, whimsical dreams, either waking or sleeping." —*The Onion*

"Brockmeier's witty, bittersweet tales are reminiscent of the work of Steven Millhauser; his stories successfully combine sophistication with innocence, lyricism with simplicity, formal quirkiness with a straightforward emotional fervency."

—Heidi Julavits, author of *The Mineral Palace*

"A dazzling collection . . . tales as dense and textured as Flannery O'Connor's." —*Arkansas Times*

"May remind some readers of certain of the beautiful classic parables of Ray Bradbury."

—Joyce Carol Oates, author of *We Were the Mulvaneys*

"[A] mixture of fantasy, magic, and astonishing point of view . . . Brockmeier speaks a unique voice."

—*Richmond Times-Dispatch*

"Kevin Brockmeier's stories are crystalline wonders. They are fairy tales: wise, magical and heartwrenching; fantastic, and also achingly real. They are breathtaking."

—Thisbe Nissen, author of *The Good People of New York*

KEVIN BROCKMEIER

Things That Fall from the Sky

Kevin Brockmeier is the author of *The Truth About Celia* and a children's book, *City of Names*. He has published stories in *The Georgia Review*, *The Carolina Quarterly*, and *McSweeney's*. His story "Space" from *Things That Fall from the Sky* has been selected for *The Best American Short Stories*, and his story "The Green Children" from *The Truth About Celia* has been selected for *The Year's Best Fantasy & Horror*. He has received the *Chicago Tribune*'s Nelson Algren Award, an Italo Calvino Short Fiction Award, a James Michener-Paul Engle Fellowship, two O. Henry Awards (one, a first prize), and most recently, a grant from the National Endowment for the Arts. He lives in Little Rock, Arkansas.

Books by Kevin Brockmeier

The Truth About Celia

Things That Fall from the Sky

City of Names

Things That Fall from the Sky

Kevin Brockmeier

Vintage Contemporaries
Vintage Books • A Division of Random House, Inc. • New York

for my mom

FIRST VINTAGE CONTEMPORARIES EDITION, JULY 2003

Published in the United States by Vintage Books, a division of Random House, Inc., New York, and simultaneously in Canada by Random House of Canada Limited, Toronto. Originally published in hardcover in slightly different form in the United States by Pantheon Books, a division of Random House, Inc., New York, in 2002.

Vintage is a registered trademark and Vintage Contemporaries and colophon are registered trademarks of Random House, Inc.

Permissions acknowledgments can be found at the end of the book.

The Library of Congress has cataloged the Pantheon edition as follows:
Brockmeier, Kevin.
Things that fall from the sky / Kevin Brockmeier
p. cm.
ISBN 0-375-42134-3
1. Psychological fiction, American. 2. Fantasy fiction, American.
I. Title.
PS3602.R63 T48 2002
813'.6—dc21 2001036222

Vintage ISBN: 0-375-72769-8

Book design by Johanna Roebas
Illustrations by Matthew Songer

www.vintagebooks.com

Printed in the United States of America
10 9 8 7 6 5 4 3 2

Contents

These Hands 3

Things That Fall from the Sky 43

Apples 68

A Day in the Life of Half of Rumpelstiltskin 85

The Ceiling 101

Small Degrees 118

The Jesus Stories 129

Space 141

The Passenger 156

The Light through the Window 184

The House at the End of the World 192

Things That Fall from the Sky

In the fairy tale an incomprehensible happiness rests upon an incomprehensible condition. A box is opened, and all evils fly out. A word is forgotten, and cities perish. A lamp is lit, and love flies away. A flower is plucked, and human lives are forfeited. An apple is eaten, and the hope of God is gone.

—G. K. CHESTERTON

These Hands

The protagonist of this story is named Lewis Winters. He is also its narrator, and he is also me. Lewis is thirty-four years old. His house is small and tidy and sparsely furnished, and the mirrors there return the image of a man inside of whom he is nowhere visible, a face within which he doesn't seem to belong: there is the turn of his lip, the knit of his brow, and his own familiar gaze: there is the promise of him, but where is he? Lewis longs for something not ugly, false, or confused. He chases the yellow-green bulbs of fireflies and cups them between his palms. He watches copter-seeds whirl from the limbs of great trees. He believes in the bare possibility of grace, in kindness and the memory of kindness, and in the fierce and sudden beauty of color. He sometimes believes that this is enough. On quiet evenings, Lewis drives past houses and tall buildings into the flat yellow grasslands that embrace the city. The black road tapers to a point, and the fields sway in the wind, and the sight of the sun dropping red past the hood of his car fills him with sadness and wonder. Lewis lives alone. He sleeps poorly. He writes fairy tales. This is not one of them.

The lover, now absent, of the protagonist of this story is named Caroline Mitchell. In the picture framed on his desk, she stands gazing into the arms of a small tree, a mittened hand at her eyes, lit by the afternoon sun as if through a screen of water. She looks puzzled and eager, as though the wind had rustled her name through the branches; in a moment, a leaf will tumble onto her forehead. Caroline is watchful and sincere, shy yet earnest. She seldom speaks, and when she does her lips scarcely part, so that sometimes Lewis must listen closely to distinguish her voice from the cycling of her breath. Her eyes are a miracle—a startled blue with frail green spokes bound by a ring of black—and he is certain that if he could draw his reflection from them, he would discover there a face neither foreign nor lost. Caroline sleeps face down, her knees curled to her chest: she sleeps often and with no sheets or blankets. Her hair is brown, her skin pale. Her smile is vibrant but brief, like a bubble that lasts only as long as the air is still. She is eighteen months old.

A few questions deserve answer, perhaps, before I continue. So then: The walls behind which I'm writing are the walls of my home—the only thing padded is the furniture, the only thing barred the wallpaper. Caroline is both alive and (I imagine—I haven't seen her now in many days) well. And I haven't read Nabokov—not ever, not once.

All this said, it's time we met, my love and I.

* * *

It was a hopeful day of early summer, and a slight, fresh breeze tangled through the air. The morning sun shone from telephone wires and the windshields of resting cars, and high clouds unfolded like the tails of galloping horses. Lewis stood before a handsome dark-brick house, flattening his shirt into his pants. The house seemed to conceal its true dimensions behind the planes and angles of its front wall. An apron of hedges stretched beneath its broad lower windows, and a flagstone walk, edged with black soil, elbowed from the driveway to the entrance. He stepped to the front porch and pressed the doorbell.

"Just a minute," called a faint voice.

Lewis turned to look along the street, resting his hand against a wooden pillar. A chain of lawns glittered with dew beneath the blue sky—those nearby green and bristling, those in the distance merely panes of white light. A blackbird lighted on the stiff red flag of a mailbox. From inside the house came the sound of a door wheeling on faulty hinges, a series of quick muffled footsteps, and then an abrupt reedy squeak. *Hello,* thought Lewis. *Hello, I spoke to you on the telephone.* The front door drew inward, stopped short on its chain, and shut. He heard the low mutter of a voice, like residual water draining through a straw. Then the door opened to reveal a woman in a billowy cotton bathrobe, the corner of its hem dark with water. A lock of black hair swept across her cheek from under the dome of a towel. In her hand she carried a yellow toy duck. "Yes?" she said.

"Hello," said Lewis. "I spoke to you on the telephone." The woman gave him a quizzical stare. "The nanny position? You asked me to stop by this morning for an interview." When she cocked an eyebrow, he withdrew a step, motioning toward his car. "If I'm early, I can—"

"Oh!" realized the woman. "Oh, yes." She smiled, tucking a few damp hairs behind the rim of her ear. "The interview. I'm sorry.

Come in." Lewis followed her past a small brown table and a rising chain of wooden banisters into the living room. A rainbow of fat plastic rings littered the silver gray carpet, and a grandfather clock ticked against the far wall. She sank onto the sofa, crossing her legs. "Now," she said, beckoning him to sit beside her. "I'm Lisa. Lisa Mitchell. And you are—?"

"Lewis Winters." He took a seat. "We spoke earlier."

"Lewis—?" Lisa Mitchell gazed into the whir of the ceiling fan, then gave a swift decisive nod. "Aaah!" she lilted, a smile softening her face. "You'll have to excuse me. It's been a hectic morning. When we talked on the phone, I assumed you were a woman. Lois, I thought you said. *Lois* Winters. We haven't had too many male applicants." Her hand fluttered about dismissively as she spoke, and the orange bill of the rubber duck she held bobbed past her cheek. "This *would* seem to explain the deep voice, though, wouldn't it?" She smoothed the sash of her bathrobe down her thigh. "So, tell me about your last job. What did you do?"

"I'm a storyteller," said Lewis.

"Pardon?"

"I wrote—write—fairy tales."

"Oh!" said Lisa. "That's good. Thomas—that's my husband, Thomas—" She patted a yawn from her lips. "Excuse me. Thomas will like that. And have you looked after children before?"

"No," Lewis answered. "No, not professionally. But I've worked with *groups* of children. I've read stories in nursery schools and libraries." His hands, which had been clasped, drew apart. "I'm comfortable with children, and I think I understand them."

"When would you be free to start?" asked Lisa.

"Tomorrow," said Lewis. "Today."

"Do you live nearby?"

"Not far. Fifteen minutes."

"Would evenings be a problem?"

"Not at all."

"Do you have a list of references?" At this Lisa closed her grip on the yellow duck, and it emitted a querulous little peep. She gave a start, then laughed, touching her free hand to her chest. She held the duck to her face as it bloomed with air. "Have I had him all this time?" she asked, thumbing its bill.

Somewhere in the heart of the house, a child began to wail. The air seemed to grow thick with discomfort as they listened. "*Some*one's cranky," said Lisa. She handed Lewis the duck as she stood. "Excuse me," she said. She hurried past a floor lamp and the broad green face of a television, then slipped away around the corner.

The grandfather clock chimed the hour as Lewis waited, its brass tail pendulating behind a tall glass door. He scratched a ring of grit from the dimple of the sofa cushion. He inspected the toy duck—its popeyes and the upsweep of its tail, the pock in the center of its flat yellow belly—then waddled it along the seam of a throw pillow. *Quack,* he thought. *Quack quack.* Lewis pressed its navel to the back of his hand, squeezing, and it constricted with a squeak; when he released it, it puckered and gripped him. He heard Lisa's voice in an adjacent room, all but indistinct above a siren-roll of weeping. "Now, now," she was saying. "Now, now." Lewis put the duck down.

When Lisa returned, a small child was gathered to her shoulder. She was wrapped in fluffy red pajamas with vinyl pads at the feet, and her slender neck rose from the wreath of a wilted collar. "Shhh," Lisa whispered, gently patting her daughter's back. "Shhh."

Lisa's hair fell unbound past her forehead, its long wet strands twisted like roads on a map. Her daughter clutched the damp towel in her hands, nuzzling it as if it were a comfort blanket. "Little Miss Grump," chirped Lisa, standing at the sofa. "Aren't you, sweetie?" Caroline fidgeted and whimpered, then began to wail again.

Lisa frowned, joggling her in the crook of her arm.

"Well," she said, "let's see how the two of you get along. Caroline—" With a thrust and a sigh, she presented her daughter, straightening her arms as if engaged in a push-up. "This is Lewis. Lewis—" And she was thrashing in my hands, muscling away from me, the weight of her like something lost and suddenly remembered: a comfort and a promise, a slack sail bellying with wind.

Her voice split the air as she twitched from side to side. Padding rustled at her waist.

"Oh, dear," said Lisa. "Maybe we'd better . . ."

But Lewis wasn't listening; instead, he drew a long heavy breath. If he could pretend himself into tears, he thought, perhaps he could calm her. For a moment as sharp as a little notched hook, he held her gaze. Then, shuddering, he burst into tears. His eyes sealed fast and his lips flared wide. With a sound like the snap and rush of a struck match, his ears opened and filled with air. Barbs of flickering blue light hovered behind his eyes. He could hear the world outside growing silent and still as he wept.

When he looked out at her, Caroline was no longer crying. She blinked out at him from wide bewildered eyes, her bottom lip folding in hesitation. Then she handed him the damp towel.

It was a gesture of sympathy—meant, Lewis knew, to reassure him—and as he draped the towel over his shoulder, a broad grin creased his face.

Lisa shook her head, laughing. "Look," she said, "Thomas and

I have plans for this evening, and we still haven't found a baby-sitter. So if you could come by around six—?"

Caroline heard the sound of laughter and immediately brightened, smiling and tucking her chin to her chest. Lewis brushed a finger across her cheek. "Of course," he said.

"Good." Lisa lifted her daughter from his arms. "We'll see how you do, and if all goes well . . ."

All did. When Lisa and Thomas Mitchell returned late that night—his keys and loose change jingling in his pocket, her perfume winging past him as she walked into the living room—Caroline was asleep in his lap. A pacifier dangled from her mouth. The television mumbled in the corner. Lewis started work the next morning.

* * *

As a matter of simple aesthetics, the ideal human form is that of the small child. We lose all sense of grace as we mature, all sense of balance and all sense of restraint. Tufts of wiry hair sprout like moss in our hollows; our cheekbones edge to an angle and our noses stiffen with cartilage; we buckle and curve, widen and purse, like a vinyl record left too long in the sun. The journey into our few core years is a journey beyond that which saw us complete. Many are the times I have wished that Caroline and I might have made this journey together. If I could, I would work my way backward, paring away the years. I would reel my life around the wheel of this longing like so much loose wire. I would heave myself past adolescence and boyhood, past infancy and birth, into the first thin parcel of my flesh and the frail white trellis of my bones. I would be a massing of tissue, a clutch of cells, and I'd meet with her on the other side. If I could, I would begin again, but nothing I've found will allow it. We survive into another and more awkward age than our own.

* * *

Caroline was sitting in a saddle-chair, its blue plastic tray freckled with oatmeal. She lifted a bright wedge of peach to her lips, and its syrup wept in loose strings from her fist to her bib. Lewis held the back of a polished silver spoon before her like a mirror. "Who's that?" he said. "Who's inside that spoon? Who's that in there?"

Caroline gazed into its dome as she chewed her peach. "Cah-line," she said.

Lewis reversed the spoon, and her reflection toppled over into its bowl. "Oh my goodness!" he said. His voice went weak with astonishment. "Caroline is standing on her head!" Caroline prodded the spoon, then taking it by the handle, her hand on his, steered it into her mouth. When she released it, Lewis peered inside. "Hey!" he said. His face grew stern. "Where did you put Caroline?" She patted her stomach, smiling, and Lewis gasped. "You *ate* Caroline!"

Caroline nodded. Her eyes, as she laughed, were as sharp and rich as light edging under a door.

The upstairs shower disengaged with a discrete shudder, and Lewis heard water suddenly gurgling through the throat of the kitchen sink. Mr. Mitchell dashed into the kitchen swinging a brown leather briefcase. He straightened his hat and drank a glass of orange juice. He skinned an apple with a paring knife. Its cortex spiraled cleanly away from the flesh and, when he left for work, it remained on the counter like a little green basket. "Six o'clock," said Mrs. Mitchell, plucking an umbrella from around a doorknob. "Seven at the outside. Think you can make it till then?" She kissed her daughter on the cheek, then waggled her earlobe with a fingertip. "Now you be a good girl, okay?" She tucked a sheaf of papers into her purse and nodded good-bye, extending her umbrella as she stepped into the morning.

That day, as a gentle rain dotted the windows, Lewis swept the kitchen and vacuumed the carpets. He dusted the roofs of dormant appliances—the oven and the toaster, the pale, serene computer. He polished the bathroom faucets to a cool silver. When Caroline knocked a pair of ladybug magnets from the refrigerator, he showed her how to nudge them across a tabletop, one with the force of the other, by pressing them pole to common pole. "You see," he said, "there's something there. It looks like nothing, but you can feel it." In the living room, they watched a sequence of animated cartoons—nimble, symphonic, awash with color. Caroline sat at the base of the television, smoothing fields of static from its screen with her palm. They read a flap-book with an inset bunny. They assembled puzzles onto sheets of corkboard. They constructed a fortress with the cushions of the sofa; when bombed with an unabridged dictionary, it collapsed like the huskwood of an old fire.

That afternoon, the sky cleared to a proud, empty blue, and Lewis walked with Caroline to the park. The children there were pitching stones into a seething brown creek, fat with new rain, and the birds that wheeled above them looked like tiny parabolic *M*'s and *W*'s. The wind smelled of pine and wet asphalt.

Lewis strapped Caroline into the bucket of a high swing. He discovered a derelict kickball between two rocking horses and, standing before her, tossed it into the tip of her swing, striking her knee, her toe, her shin. "Do it again," she said as the force of her momentum shot the ball past his shoulder, or sent it soaring like a loose balloon into the sky. It disappeared, finally, into a nest of brambles. Pushing Caroline from behind, Lewis watched her arc away from him and back, pausing before her return like a roller-toy he'd once concocted from a coffee can and a rubber band. She weighed so little, and he knew that if he chose, he could propel her around the axle of the swing set, a single robust shove spinning her like a second hand from twelve to twelve to twelve. Instead, he let her swing to a stop, her arms falling limp from the chains as she slowed. A foam sandal dangled uncertainly from her big toe. Her head lolled onto her chest. She was, suddenly, asleep. As Lewis lifted her from the harness, she relaxed into a broad yawn, the tip of her tongue settling gently between her teeth. He carried her home.

After he had put her to bed, Lewis drew the curtains against the afternoon sun and pulled a small yellow table to her side. He sat watching her for a moment. Her breath sighed over her pillowcase, the turn of fabric nearest her lips flitting slightly with each exhalation. She reached for a stuffed bear, cradling it to her heart, and her eyes began to jog behind their lids. Gingerly, Lewis pressed a finger to one of them. He could feel it twitching at his touch like a chick rolling over in its egg. What could she be dreaming, he wondered, and would she remember when she woke? How could something so close be so hidden? And how was it that in the light of such a question we could each of us hold out hope—search eyes as dark as winter for the flicker of intimacy, dream of seizing one another in a fit of recognition? As he walked silently from her bedroom, Lewis lifted from the toy shelf a red plastic See 'n' Say, its face wreathed with calling animals. In the hallway, he trained its index on the picture of a lion, depressing the lever cocked at its frame. *This,* said the machine, *is a robin,* and it whittered a little aria. When he turned the dial to a picture of a lamb on a tussock of grass, it said the same thing. Dog and pony, monkey and elephant: *robin—twit twit whistle.* Lewis set the toy against a wall, listening to the cough of a receding car. He passed through the dining room and climbed the back stairway, wandered the deep and inviolate landscape of the house—solemn with the thought of faulty lessons, and of how often we are shaped in this way.

* * *

An old story tells of a man who grew so fond of the sky—of the clouds like hills and the shadows of hills, of the birds like notes of music and the stars like distant blessings—that he made of his heart a kite and sailed it into the firmament. There he felt the high mechanical tug of the air. The sunlight rushed through him, and the sharp blue wind, and the world seemed a far and a learnable thing. His gaze (the story continues) he tied like a long string to his heart, and never looking down, lest he pull himself to earth, he wandered the world ever after in search of his feet.

Talking about love, I suspect, is much like this story. What is it, then, that insists that we make the attempt? The hope of some new vision? The drive for words and order? We've been handed a map whose roads lead to a place we understand: *Now,* says a voice, *disentangle them.* And though we fear that we will lose our way, still, there is this wish to try. Perhaps, though, if we allow our perceptions of love to brighten and fade as they will, allow it even if they glow no longer than a spark launched from a fire, perhaps we will not pull our heart from its course: surely this is possible.

My love, then, for Caroline is what slows me into sleep at night. It is a system of faith inhabiting some part of me that's deeper than I've traveled. The thought of her fills me with comfort and balance, like heat spilling from the floor register of an old building. Her existence at this moment, alongside me in time, unhesitating and sure, all of this, the *now* of her, is what stirs through me when I fail. My love for Caroline is the lens through which I see the world, and the world through that lens is a place whose existence addresses my own.

Caroline chews crayons, red like a fire truck, green like a river, silver like the light from a passing airplane, and there's something in my love for her that speaks this same urge: I want to receive the world inside me. My love for Caroline is the wish that we might spend our lives together: marry in a hail of rice, watch the childhood of our children disappear, and think to ourselves someday: when this person is gone, no one in all the world will remember the things I remember.

Salient point is an early and sadly obsolete term for the heart as it first appears in the embryo: I fell upon it in a book of classical obstetrics with a sense of celebration. The heart, I believe, is that point where we merge with the universe. It is salient as a jet of water is salient, leaping continually upward, and salient as an angle is salient, its vertex projecting into this world, its limbs fanning out behind the frame of another. What I love of Caroline is that space of her at rest behind the heart, true and immanent, hidden and vast, the arc that this angle subtends.

I would like to cobble such few sentences into a tower, placing them in the world, so that I might absorb what I can of these things in a glance. But when we say *I love you,* we say it not to shape the world. We say it because there's a wind singing through us that knows it to be true, and because even when we speak them without shrewdness or understanding, it is good, we know, to say these things.

* * *

The dishwasher thrummed in the kitchen, and the thermostat ticked in the hallway, and the tumble-drier called from the basement like a tittupping horse. Caroline lay on the silver-gray carpet, winking each eye in turn as she scrutinized her thumb. Her hair was drawn through the teeth of a barrette, and the chest of her shirt was pulled taut beneath one arm. Lewis could see her heartbeat welling through the gate of her ribs. It called up in him the memory of a time when, as a schoolboy, his teacher had allowed him to hold the battery lamp during a power failure. He had lain on the floor, balancing the lamp atop his chest, and everywhere in the slate black schoolroom the light had pulsed with his heart. Like a shaken belief or a damaged affection, the life within such a moment could seem all but irreclaimable.

The seconds swayed past in the bob weight of the grandfather clock.

"Come here," said Lewis, beckoning to Caroline, and when she'd settled into his lap, he told her this story: In a town between a forest and the sea there lived a clever and gracious little girl. She liked to play with spoons and old buttons, to swat lump-bugs and jump over things, and her name was Caroline.

("I don' like *spoons,*" said Caroline. *Spoons?* said Lewis. *Did I say spoons? I meant goons.* Caroline giggled and shook her head. "No-*o*." *Prunes?* "Nuh-uh." *Baboons?* Caroline paused to consider this, her finger paddling lazily against her shirt collar. "Okay.")

So then: Caroline, who played with buttons and baboons, had all the hours from sun to moon to wander the city as she wished, scratching burrs from her socks or thumping dandelion heads. The grown-ups offered her but one caution: if ever the sky should threaten rain, the clouds begin to grumble, or the wind blow suddenly colder, she must hurry indoors. The grown-ups had good reason to extend such a warning, for the town in which they lived was made entirely of soap. It had been whittled and sliced from the Great Soap Mountains. There were soaphouses and soapscrapers, chains of soap lampposts above wide soap roadways, and in the town center, on a pedestal of marbled soap, a rendering of a soapminer, his long proud shovel at his side. Sometimes, when the dark sky ruptured and the rains came daggering across the land, those of the town who had not taken shelter, the tired and the lost, the poky and the dreamy, would vanish, never to return. "Washed clean away," old-timers would declare, nodding sagely.

One day, Caroline was gathering soapberries from a glade at the lip of the forest. Great somber clouds, their bellies black with rain, had been weltering in from the ocean for hours, but she paid them no mind: she had raced the rain before, and she could do it again. When a cloud discharged a hollow growl, she thought it was her stomach, hungry for soapberries, and so ate a few. When the wind began to swell and chill, she simply zipped up her jacket. She bent to place a berry in her small blue hat, and felt her skin pimpling at the nape of her neck, and when she stood again, the rain was upon her.

Caroline fled from the forest. She arrowed past haystacks and canting trees, past empty pavilions and blinking red stoplights. A porch gate wheeled on its hinges and slammed against a ventilation tank. A lamplight burst in a spray of orange sparks. *Almost,* thought Caroline, as her house, then her door, then the glowspeck of her doorbell came into view. And at just that moment, as she blasted past the bakery to her own front walk, a tremendous drift of soapsuds took hold of her from behind, whipping her up and toward the ocean.

When Caroline awoke, the sunlight was lamping over her weary body. Her skin was sticky with old soap. Thin whorls of air iridesced all around her. She shook her head, unfolded in a yawn, and watched a bluebird flap through a small round cloud beneath her left elbow. That was when she realized: she was bobbing through the sky inside a bubble! She tried to climb the inside membrane of the vessel, but it rolled her onto her nose. She prodded its septum with her finger and it stretched and recoiled, releasing a few airy driblets of soap that popped when she blew on them. *Bubble, indeed,* she thought, indignant, arms akimbo. Caroline (though a clever and a gracious little girl) could not think of a single solution to her dilemma, for if her craft were to burst she would surely fall to earth, and if she fell to earth she would shatter like a snowball, so she settled into the bay of her bubble, watching the sky and munching the soapberries from her small blue hat.

There is little to see from so high in the air: clouds and stars and errant birds; the fields and the hills, the rivers and highways, as small and distinct as the creases in your palm. There is a time as the morning brightens when the lakes and rivers, catching the first light, will go silvering through the quiet black land. And in the evening, when the sun drops, a flawless horizon will prism its last flare into a haze of seven colors. Once, Caroline watched a man's heart sail by like a kite, once a golden satellite swerving past the moon. Preoccupied birds sometimes flew straight toward her, their wings stiff and open, their beaks like drawn swords, yawing away before they struck her bubble. On a chilly afternoon, an airplane passed so close that she counted nineteen passengers gaping at her through its windows, their colorless faces like a series of stills on a filmstrip. And on a delicate, breezy morning, as she stared through a veining of clouds at the land, Caroline noticed that the twists of color had faded from the walls of her bubble. Then, abruptly, it burst.

Caroline found herself plummeting like a buzz bomb from the sky, the squares of far houses growing larger and larger. Her hair strained upward against the fall, tugging at her scalp. Her cheeks beat like pennants in the wind. She shut her eyes. As for what became of her, no one is certain, or rather there are many tales, and many tellers, each as certain as the last. Some say she spun into the arms of a startled baboon, who raised her in the forest on coconuts and turnip roots. Some say she dropped onto the Caroline Islands, striking the beach in a spasm of sand, and so impressed the islanders with the enthusiasm of her arrival that with a mighty shout they proclaimed her Minister of Commerce. And some say she landed in this very house, on this very couch, in this very room, where I told her this story and put her to bed.

* * *

The human voice is an extraordinary thing: an alliance of will and breath that, without even the fastening of hands, can forge for us a home in other people. Air is sent trembling through the frame of the mouth, and we find ourselves admitted to some far, unlikely country: this must, I think, be regarded as nothing short of wondrous. The first voice I remember hearing belonged, perhaps, to a stranger or a lost relation, for I cannot place it within my family: it sounded like a wooden spool rolling on a wooden floor. My father had a voice like cement revolving in a drum, my mother like the whirring of many small wings. My own, I've been told, resembles the rustling of snow against a windowpane. What must the mother's voice, beneath the whisper of her lungs, beneath the little detonations of her heartbeat, sound like to the child in the womb? A noise without design or implication, as heedless as growth, as mechanical as thunder? Or the echo of some nascent word come quaking through the body? Is it the first intimation of another life cradling our own, a sign that suggests that this place is a someone? Or do children, arriving from some other, more insistent landscape, need such testimony? If the human voice itself does not evince a living soul, then that voice raised in song surely must.

Things go right, things go wrong
hearts may break but not for long
you will grow up proud and strong
sleepy little baby.

Of all the forms of voice and communion, a song is perhaps the least mediated by the intellect. It ropes its way through the tangle of our cautions, joining singer to listener like a vine between two trees. I once knew a man whose heart percussed in step with the music that he heard; he would not listen to drums played in hurried or irregular cadence; he left concerts and dances and parties, winced at passing cars, and telephoned his neighbors when they played their stereos too loudly, in the fear that with each unsteady beat he might malfunction. Song is an exchange exactly that immediate and physiological. It attests to the life of the singer through our skin and through our muscles, through the wind in our lungs and the fact of our own beating heart. The evidence of other spirits becomes that of our own body. Speech is sound shaped into meaning through words, inflection, and modulation. Music is sound shaped into meaning through melody, rhythm, and pitch. A song arises at the point where these two forces collide. But such an encounter can occur in more than one place.

Where, then, is song most actual and rich—in the singer or in the audience?

Dream pretty dreams
touch beautiful things
let all the skies surround you
swim with the swans
and believe that upon
some glorious dawn
love will find you.

A successful song comes to sing itself inside the listener. It is cellular and seismic, a wave coalescing in the mind and in the flesh. There is a message outside and a message inside, and those messages are the same, like the pat and thud of two heartbeats, one within you, one surrounding. The message of the lullaby is that it's okay to dim the eyes for a time, to lose sight of yourself as you sleep and as you grow: if you drift, it says, you'll drift ashore: if you fall, you will fall into place.

And if you see some old fool
who looks like a friend
tell him good night old man
my friend.

* * *

Lewis stood with a washcloth before Caroline's highchair, its tray white with milk from a capsized tumbler. A streetlamp switched on outside the kitchen window, and as he turned to look, another did the same. The sun had left channels of pink and violet across the sky, in which a few wavering stars were emerging. He could hear the rush of commuter traffic behind the dry autumn clicking of leaves, motor horns calling forlornly, a siren howling in the distance. The highchair stood like a harvest crab on its thin silver stilts. Lewis sopped the milk up from its tray and brushed the crumbs from its seat, rinsing his washcloth at the gurgling sink. All around the city, he thought, staring into the twilight, streetlamps were brightening one by one, generating warm electric purrs and rings of white light. From far above, as they blinked slowly on and off, they would look like rainwater striking the lid of a puddle.

In the living room, Caroline sat at the foot of the television, several inches from the screen, watching a small cartoon Martian chuckle perniciously as he fashioned an enormous ray gun. Lewis knelt beside her and, just for a moment, saw the black egg of the Martian's face shift beneath his gleaming helmet—but then his eyes began to tingle, and his perception flattened, and it was only a red-green-blueness of phosphorescent specks and the blade of his own nose. He flurried his hand through Caroline's hair, then pinched a dot of cookie from her cheek. "Sweetie," he said to her, standing. When his knees cracked, she started.

A set of cardboard blocks, red and blue and thick as bread loaves, were clustered before a reclining chair. They looked like something utterly defeated, a grove of pollard trees or the frame of a collapsed temple. Earlier in the day, Lewis had played a game with Caroline in which he stacked them two on two to the ceiling and she charged them, arms swinging, until they toppled to the carpet. Each time she rushed them, she would rumble like a speeding truck. Each time they fell she would laugh with excitement, bobbing up and down in a stiff little dance. She rarely tired of this game. As often as not, actually, she descended upon the structure in a sort of ambush before it was complete: Lewis would stoop to collect another block, hear the drum of running feet, and down they would go. Now, as she peered at the television, he stacked the blocks into two narrow columns, each its own color, and bridged them carefully at the peak; satisfied, he lapsed onto the sofa.

Propping his glasses against his forehead, he yawned and pressed his palms to his eyes. Grains of light sailed through the darkness, like snow surprised by a headlamp, and when he looked out at the world again, Caroline had made her way to his side. She flickered her hands and burbled a few quick syllables, her arms swaying above her like the runners of a sea plant: in her language of blurt and gesture, this meant *carry me,* or *hold me,* or *pick me up,* and swinging into her Lewis did just that. She stood in his lap, balancing with one smooth-socked foot on either thigh, and reached for his forehead. "Lasses," she said. Lewis removed his glasses, handing them to her, and answered, "That's right." An ice-white bloom of television flashed from each lens as Caroline turned them around in her palms. When she pressed them to her face, the stems floated inches from her ears; then they slipped past her nose and hitched around her shoulders, hanging there like a necklace or a bow tie. Lewis felt himself smiling as he retrieved them. He polished them on the tail of his shirt and returned them to their rightful perch.

He looked up to find Caroline losing her balance, foundering toward him. Her foot slid off his leg onto the sofa and her arms lurched up from her side. "Whoa," he said, catching her. "You okay?" She tottered back onto his lap, her head pressing against his cheek. He could feel the dry warmth of her skin, the arching of her eyebrows, the whiffet of her breath across his face. Then, straightening, she kissed him. The flat of her tongue passed up his chin and over his lips, and, stopping at his nose, inverted and traveled back down. Lewis could feel it tensed against him like a spring, and when it swept across the crest of his lips, he lightly kissed its tip. Caroline closed her mouth with a tiny pecking sound. She sniffled, brushed her nose, and settled into him. "Glasses," she said, and her warm brown hair fell against his collarbone. Lewis blinked and touched a finger to his dampened chin. His ears were tingling as if from a breeze. His head was humming like a long flat roadway.

From the front porch came the rattle of house keys. As the lock bolt retracted with a ready chink, Caroline dropped to his lap. She turned to watch the television and pillowed her head on his stomach.

"Home!" called Mr. Mitchell, and the door clapped shut behind him.

* * *

My brother is three years my senior. When I was first learning to speak, he was the only person to whom my tongue taps and labial stops seemed a language. I would dispense a little train of stochastic syllables—*pa ba mi da,* for instance, and he would translate, for the benefit of my parents: *He wants some more applesauce.* My brother understood me, chiefly, from basic sympathy and the will to understand: the world, I am certain, responds to such forces. It was in this fashion that I knew what Caroline told me, though when she said it she was mumbling up from sleep, and though it sounded to the ear as much like *igloo* or *allegory,* when with a quiet and perfect affection she said, "I love you."

* * *

With fingers spidery-weak from the cold, Lewis worked the tag of Caroline's zipper into its slide, fastening her jacket with a tidy *zzzt.* He tightened her laces, straightened her mittens, and wiped her nose with a tissue. He adjusted her socks and trousers and the buttonless blue puff of her hood. "All right," he said, patting her back. "Off you go." Caroline scampered for the sandbox, her hood flipping from her head to bob along behind her. When she crossed its ledge, she stood for a moment in silence. Then she growled like a bear and gave an angry stamp, felling a hillock of abandoned sand. Lewis watched her from a concrete bench. She found a small pink shovel and arranged a mound of sand into four piles, one at each rail, as if ladling out soup at a dinner table. She buried her left foot and kicked a flurry of grit onto the grass.

Brown leaves shot with threads of red and yellow skittered across the park. They swept past merry-go-rounds and picnic tables, past heavy gray stones and rotunda bars. A man and his daughter tottered on a seesaw, a knot of sunlight shuttling along the rod between them like a bubble in a tube of water. Two boys were bouncing tennis balls in the parking lot, hurling them against the asphalt and watching them leap into the sky, and another was descending a decrepit wire fence, its mesh of tendons loose and wobbling. Caroline sat on her knees in the sandbox, burrowing: she unearthed leaves and acorns and pebbles, a shiny screw-top bottlecap and her small pink shovel. A boy with freckles and cowboy boots joined her with a grimace, a ring of white diaper peering from above his pants. His mother handed him a plastic bucket, tousling his plume of tall red hair. "Now you play nice," she told him, and sat next to Lewis on the bench. She withdrew a soda can from her purse, popping its tab and sipping round the edge of its lid. Caroline placed her bottlecap in her shovel, then scolded it, *no, no, no,* and tipped it to the side. The woman on the bench turned to Lewis, gesturing cheerily, nonchalantly. "Your daughter is a*dor*able," she said.

For a moment Lewis didn't know how to respond. He felt a strange coldness shivering up from inside him: it was as if his body were a window, suddenly unlatched, and beyond it was the hard aspen wind of December. Then the sensation dwindled, and his voice took hold of him. "Thanks," he said. "She's not mine, but thank you."

The woman crossed her legs, tapping her soda can with a lacquered red fingernail. "So," she asked, "you're an uncle, then?"

"Sitter."

From the back of her throat came a high little interrogatory *mm.* In the sandbox, her son slid his plastic bucket over his head. *Echo,* he hollered, his face concealed in its trough: *echo, echo, echo.* He was the sort of boy one might expect to find marching loudly into weddings and libraries, chanting the theme songs from television comedies and striking a metal pan with a wooden spoon. "I'm Brooke," said the woman, bending to set her soda can at her feet. "And you are—?"

"Lewis."

She nodded, then rummaged in her purse, a sack of brown woven straw as large as a bed pillow. "Would you like some gum, Lewis? I know it's in here somewhere." Her son lumbered over to Caroline and clapped his bucket over her head. It struck with a loud thumping sound. Lewis, watching, stepped to her side and removed it, then hoisted her to his shoulder as she began to cry.

The woman on the bench glanced up from her purse. "Alex*ander,*" she exclaimed. She stomped to the sandbox in counterfeit anger.

"*What* did you do?" The boy glowered, his mouth pinching shut like the spiracle of a balloon. He threw the small pink shovel at a litter bin and began punching his left arm. "*That* settles it," said his mother, pointing. "No more fits today from *you,* mister. To the car."

"Your bucket," said Lewis—it was dangling from his right hand, fingers splayed against Caroline's back.

"Thanks," said the woman, hooking it into her purse. She waved as she left with her son.

Caroline was nuzzling against his neck, her arm folded onto her stomach. Her chest rose and fell against his own, and Lewis relaxed his breathing until they were moving in concert. He walked to a wooden picnic table and sat on its top, brushing a few pine needles to the ground. The wind sighed through the trees, and the creek rippled past beneath a ridge of grass. Silver minnows paused and darted through its shallows, kinks of sunlight agitating atop the water like a sort of camouflage for their movements. Lewis tossed a pine cone into the current and watched it sail, scales flared and glistening, through a tiny cataract. An older couple, arms intertwined, passed by with their adolescent daughter. "I'm not sure I even *believe* in peace of mind," the girl was saying, her hands fluttering at her face as if to fend off a fly.

He could hear Caroline slurping on her thumb. "You awake?" he asked, and she mumbled in affirmation. "Do you want to go home or do you want to stay here and play for a while?"

"Play," said Caroline.

Lewis planted her on her feet and, taking her by the hand, walked with her to the playground. A framework of chutes and tiered platforms sat in a bed of sand and gravel, and they climbed a net of ropes into its gallery. A steering wheel was bolted to a crossbeam at the forward deck, and when Caroline spun it, they beeped like horns and *whoa*ed from side to side. They snapped clots of sand from a handrail. They ran across a step-bridge swaying on its chains. A broad gleaming slide descended from a wooden shelf, its ramp speckled with dents and abrasions, and ascending a ladder to its peak, they swooped to the earth. They jumped from a bench onto an old brown stump and climbed a hill of painted rubber tires. They wheeled in slow circles on a merry-go-round, watching the world drift away and return—slide tree parking lot, slide tree parking lot—until their heads felt dizzy and buoyant, like the hollow metal globes that quiver atop radio antennas. Beside a bike rack and a fire hydrant, they discovered the calm blue mirror of a puddle; when Lewis breached it with a stone, they watched themselves pulse across the surface, wavering into pure geometry. A spray of white clouds hovered against the sky, and an airplane drifted through them with a respiratory hush. "Look," said Lewis, and Caroline followed the line of his finger. Behind the airplane were two sharp white condensation trails, cloven with blue sky, that flared and dwindled like the afterlight of a sparkler. Watching, Lewis was seized with a sudden and inexplicable sense of presence, as if weeks and miles of surrounding time and space had contracted around this place, this moment. "My God," he said, and filled his lungs with the rusty autumn air. "Look what we can do."

A man with a stout black camera was taking pictures of the playground equipment. He drew carefully toward the slide and the seesaw, the monkey bars and tire swings, altering his focus and releasing the shutter. Each print emerged from a vent at the base of the camera, humming into sight on a square of white paper. Lewis approached the man and, nodding to Caroline, asked if he might borrow the device for a moment. "Just one picture?" he asked, his head cocked eagerly. "Well," said the man, and he shrugged, giving a little flutter with his index finger. "Okay. One." Caroline had wandered in pursuit of a whirling leaf to the foot of a small green cypress tree. Its bough was pierced with the afternoon sunlight, and she gazed into the crook of its lowest branches. A flickertail squirrel lay there batting a cone. She raised a mittened hand to her eyes, squinting, and when Lewis snapped her picture, a leaf tumbled onto her forehead.

"Your daughter," said the man, collecting his camera, "is very pretty."

Lewis stared into the empty white photograph. "Thank you," he said. He blew across its face until the dim gray ghost of a tree appeared. "She is."

* * *

Though it often appears in my memories and dreams, I have not returned to the playground in many days. It is certain to have changed, however minutely, and this is what keeps me away. Were I to visit, I might find the rocking horse rusted on its heavy iron spring, the sidewalk marked with the black prints of leaves, the swings wrapped higher around their crossbars, and though they seem such small things, I'd rather not see them. The sand may have spilled past the lip of the sandbox, and the creek may have eaten away at its banks. The cypress tree might have been taken by a saw or risen a few inches closer to the sun. Perhaps a pair of lovers have carved their signet into its bark, a heart and a cross, or a square of initials. My fear, though, is that the park has simply paled with all its contents into an embryonic white; that, flattening like a photograph too long exposed, it has curled at its edges and blown away. In my thoughts, though, it grows brighter each day, fresher and finer and more distinct, away from my remembering eyes.

* * *

Caroline was nestled in bubbles. Sissing white hills of them gathered and rose, rolling from the faucet to each bank of the tub. They streamed like clouds across the water, rarefying as they accumulated, as those bubbles in the center, collapsing, coalesced into other, slightly larger bubbles, which themselves collapsed into still larger bubbles, and those into still larger (as if a cluster of grapes were to become, suddenly, one large grape), which, bursting, opened tiny chutes and flumes to the exterior, and there sat Caroline, hidden in the thick of them, the tips of her hair afloat on the surface. When she scissored her feet, the great mass of the bubbles swayed atop the water. When she twitched her arm, a little boat of froth released itself from the drift, sailing through the air into a box of tissues. She looked as if she had been planted to her shoulders in snow.

Lewis shut the water off, and the foam that had been rippling away from the head of the tub spread flat, like folds of loose skin drawing suddenly taut. The silence of the faucet left the bathroom loud with hums and whispers, and intimate noises were made vibrant and bold: effervescing bubbles, gentle whiffs of breath, metal pipes ticking in the walls. Caroline leaned forward and blew a cove the size of her thumb into a mound of bubbles. The bathwater, swaying with her motion, rocked the mound back upon her, and when she blinked up from inside it, her face was wreathed in white. Lewis pinched the soap from her eyelashes. He dried her face with a hand towel—brushed the swell of her cheeks and the bead of her nose—and dropped her rubber duck into the bubbles. It struck the water with a *ploop,* then emerged from the glittering suds. "Wack, wack," said Caroline, as it floated into her collarbone. She pulled it to the floor of the tub and watched it hop to the surface.

Lewis squirted a dollop of pink shampoo into his palm and worked it through the flurry of her hair. Its chestnut brown, darkened with water, hung in easy curves along her neck and her cheek and in the dip of skin behind each ear. His fingers, lacing through it, looked as white as slants of moonlight. He flared and collapsed them, rubbing the shampoo into a rich lather, and touched the odd runnel of soap from her forehead. One day, as he was bathing her, a bleb of shampoo had streamed into her eye, and she had kept a hand pressed to it for the rest of the day, quailing away from him whenever he walked past. Ever since then, he had been careful to roll the soap back from her face as it thickened, snapping it into the tub. When it came time to rinse, Caroline tilted her head back and shut her eyes so tightly that they shivered. Lewis braced her in the water, his palm against the smooth of her back.

With a green cotton washcloth and a bar of flecked soap, he washed her chin and her jaw, her round dimpled elbows, the small of her back and the spine of her foot. His sleeves were drawn to his upper arms, his fingertips slowly crimping. His hands passed from station to station with careful diligent presses and strokes. Caroline paddled her duck through the water, then squeezed it and watched the air bubble from under its belly. He washed her arms and her legs and the soft small bowl of her stomach. He washed the hollows of her knees, soaped her neck and soaped her chest, and felt her heart, the size of a robin's egg, pounding beneath him. Her heart, he thought, was driving her blood, and her blood was sustaining her cells, and her cells were investing her body with time. He washed her shoulder blades and the walls of her torso and imagined them expanding as she grew: her muscles would band and bundle, her bones flare open like the frame of an umbrella. He washed the shallow white shoulders that would take on curve and breadth, the waist that would taper, the hips that would round. The vents and breaches, valleys and slopes, that would become as rare and significant to some new husband as they now were to him. The face that, through the measure of its creases, would someday reveal by accident what it now revealed by intent: the feelings that were traveling through her life. He washed her fragile, dissilient, pink-fingered hands. The hands that would unfold and color with age. The hands that would learn how to catch a ball and knot a shoelace, how to hold a pencil and unlock a door, how to drive a car, how to wave farewell, how to shake hello. The hands that would learn how to touch another person, how to carry a child, and on some far day how to die.

The water was lapping against the wall of the tub. Lewis found himself gazing into the twitch of his reflection: his lips and eyes were tense with thought beside a reef of dissipating bubbles. Caroline watched for a moment, then splashed him with a palm of cupped water. When Lewis looked at her through the tiny wet globes that dotted his glasses, she laughed, and he felt some weary thing inside of him ascend and disperse, like fog lifting from a bay. He polished his glasses and his mouth curled into a smile.

When he pulled the bath plug, Caroline started, surprised, as she often was, by the sudden deep gurgle and surge. He welcomed her into the wings of a towel as the water serpent-whirled down the drain.

* * *

Sums

Number of days we spent together: 144. Number of days we spent apart (supposing that Archbishop James Usher of Meath, who calculated the date of the Creation at 23 October 4004 B.C., was correct): 2,195,195. Number of days since I last saw her: 43. Number of days since I began writing this story: 3. Number of days in her life thus far: 613. Number of days in mine thus far: 12,418; projected: 12,419. Number of times we walked to the park: 102. Number of swings on the swing set there: 3; strap swings: 2; bucket swings: 1. Number of times she rode the bucket swing: 77; the strap swing: 1. Number of times she rode the strap swing and fell: 1. Number of times I pushed her on the bucket swing, average per session: 22; total: 1,694. Number of puzzles we constructed: 194. Number of towers we assembled from large cardboard blocks: 112; demolished: 111. Number of stories I told: 58. Number of diapers I changed: 517. Number of lullabies I sang: 64. Number of days I watched, while Caroline napped, Caroline: 74; the television: 23; the sky: 7. Number of times, since we met, that I've laundered my clothing: 93; that I've finished a book: 19; that I've heard songs on the radio with her name in them: 17 (*good times never felt so good*: 9; *where did your long hair go?*: 2; a song I don't know whose chorus chants *Caroline Caroline Caroline* in a voice like the clittering of dice in a cup: 6). Number of foot-long sandwiches I've eaten since we met: 12. Number of Lewises it would take to equal in height the number of foot-long sandwiches I've eaten since we met: 2.1; number of Carolines: 4.9. Number of times I've thought today about the color of my walls: 2; about the shape of my chin: 1; about airplanes: 4; about mirrors: 3; about the inset mirror in one of Caroline's flap-books: 1; about Caroline and the turn of her lips: 6; about Caroline and macaroni and cheese: 1; about how difficult it can be to separate one thought from another: 1; about Caroline and moths and childhood fears: 4; about my childhood fear of being drawn through the grate of an escalator: 1; about my childhood fear of being slurped down the drain of a bathtub: 2; about eyes: 9; about hands: 6, about hands, mine: 3. Number of lies I've told you: 2. Number of lies I've told you about my behavior toward Caroline: 0; about fairy tales: 0; about Nabokov: 1. Number of times I've dreamt about her: 14; pleasant: 12. Number of times I've dreamt about her mother: 3; nightmares: 3. Number of nightmares I recall having had in my life: 17. Number of hours I've spent this month: 163; in vain: 163.

* * *

Lewis tidied the house while Caroline napped, gathering her toys from the kitchen and the bathroom, the stairway and the den. He collected them in the fold of his arms and quietly assembled them on her toy shelves. Warm air breathed from the ceiling vents and sunlight ribboned in through the living room windows, striking in its path a thousand little whirling constellations of dust. Lewis pulled a xylophone trolley from under the couch. He stacked rainbow quoits onto a white peg. He carried a pinwheel and a rag doll from the hallway and slipped a set of multiform plastic blocks into the multiform sockets of a block box. He walked from the oven to the coatrack, from the coatrack to the grandfather clock, fossicking about for the last of a set of three tennis balls, and, finding it behind the laundry hamper, he pressed it into its canister. Then he held the canister to his face, breathing in its flat clean scent before he shelved it in the closet of the master bedroom. Lewis often felt, upon entering this room, as if he had discovered a place that was not an aspect of the house that he knew—someplace dark and still and barren: a cavern or a sepulcher, a tremendous empty seashell. The venetian blinds were always sealed, the curtains drawn shut around them, and both were overshadowed by a fat gray oak tree. The ceiling lamp cast a dim orange light, nebular and sparse, over the bed and the dressers and the carpet. Lewis fell back on the bedspread. The cable of an electric blanket bore into his shoulder, and his head lay in a shallow channel in the center of the mattress, formed, he presumed, by the weight of a sleeping body. He yawned, drumming his hand on his chest, and listened to the sigh of a passing car. He gazed into the tiny red eye of a smoke alarm.

When he left to look in on Caroline, he found her sleeping contentedly, her thumb in her mouth. A stuffed piglet curled from beneath her, its pink snout and the tabs of its ears brushing past her stomach. Her back rose and fell like a parachute tent. He softly shut her door. Returning to the living room, he bent to place a stray red checker in his shirt pocket, then straightened and gave a start: her mother was there, sitting on the sofa and blinking into space. Lisa Mitchell rarely arrived home before the moon was as sharp as a blade in the night sky, never once before evening. Now she sat clutching a small leather purse in her lap, and a stream of sunlight delineated each thread of her hair. It was mid-afternoon.

"Early day?" asked Lewis. He removed a jack-in-the-box from the arm of a chair, sealing the lid on its unsprung clown. Lisa Mitchell neither moved nor spoke; she simply held her purse and stared. "Hello?" he tested. She sat motionless, queerly mute, like a table lamp or a podium. Then her shoulders gave a single tight spasm, as if an insect had buzzed onto the nape of her neck, and her eyes glassed with tears. Lewis felt, suddenly, understanding and small and human. "Do you need anything?" he asked. "Some water?" Lisa drew a quick high breath and nodded.

Lewis rinsed a glass in the kitchen sink, then filled it from a bay on the door of the refrigerator, watching the crushed ice and a finger of water issue from a narrow spout. When he handed it to Lisa, she sipped until her mouth pooled full, swallowed, and placed it on a side-table. Her fingertips left transparent annulets across the moist bank of the glass, her lips a wine-red crescent at its rim. Lewis sat next to her on the sofa. "Do you want to talk about it?" he asked. His voice had become as gentle as the aspiration of the ceiling-vents.

"I . . . ," said Lisa, and the corner of her mouth twitched. "He said I. . . ." Her throat gave out a little clicking noise. She trifled with the apron of her purse—snapping it open and shut, open and shut. "I lost my job," she said. And at this she sagged in on herself, shaking, and began to weep. Her head swayed, and her back lurched, and she pressed her hands to her eyes. When Lewis touched a finger to her arm, she fell against him, quaking.

"It's okay," he said. "It will all be okay." Resting against his shoulder, Lisa cried and shivered and slowly grew still. Her purse dropped to the floor as she relaxed into a sequence of calm, heavy breaths. Then, abruptly, she was crying once again. She wavered in this way—between moments of peace and trepidation—for what seemed an hour, as the white midday light slowly windowed across the carpet. After she had fallen quiet, Lewis held her and listened to her breathing. (She sighed placidly, flurrying puffs of air through her nose; she freed a little string of hiccups that seemed both deeply organic and strangely mechanical.) The sleeve of his shirt, steeped with her tears, was clinging to his upper arm, and his hand was pin-pricking awake on her back. He could feel the warm pressure of her head against his collarbone. When she shifted on the cushions, he swallowed, listening to the drumbeat of his heart. He slid his fingers over the rungs of her spine, smoothing the ripples from her blouse, and she seemed to subside into the bedding of the sofa. It was as if she were suddenly just a weight within her clothing, suspended by a hanger from his shoulder, and he thought for a moment that she had fallen asleep—but, when she blinked, he felt the soft flicker of her eye-lashes against his neck. Her stockings, sleek and coffee-brown, were beginning to ladder at the knee, and Lewis reached to touch a ravel of loose nylon. He found himself instead curling a hand through her hair.

Lisa lifted her head, looking him in the eye, as his fingers swept across a rise in her scalp. He felt her breath mingling with his. Her eyes, drawing near, were azure-blue, and walled in black, and staring into his own. They seemed to hover before him like splashes of reflected light, and Lewis wondered what they saw. The tip of her nose met with his, and when she licked her lips, he felt her tongue glance across his chin. His lips were dry and tingling, his stomach as tight as a seed pod. When his hand gave a reflexive flutter on her back, Lisa stiff-ened.

She tilted away from him, blinking, the stones of her teeth press-ing into her lip. The grandfather clock voiced three vibrant chimes, and she stood and planed her blouse into the waist of her skirt.

When she looked down upon him, her eyes were like jigsawed glass. "I think you'd better go now," she said.

* * *

Certain places are penetrated with elements of the human spirit. They act as concrete demonstrations of our hungers and capacities. A sud-den field in the thick of a forest is a place like reverence, a stand of corn a place like knowledge, a clock tower a place like fury. I have wit-nessed this and know it to be true. Caroline's house was a place like memory, a place, in fact, like my memory of her: charged with hope and loss and fascination. As I stepped each morning through her front door, I saw the wall peg hung with a weathered felt hat, the ceiling dotted with stucco, the staircase folding from floor to floor, and it was as if these things were quickened with both her presence and her ultimate departure. The stationary bicycle with its whirring front fan-wheel and the dining room table with its white lace spread, the desk cup bristling with pencils and pens and the books shelved neatly between ornamental bookends: they were the hills and trees and markers of a landscape that harbored and kept her. The windows were the windows whose panes she would print with her fingers. The doorstop was the doorstop whose spring she would flitter by its crown. The lamps were the lamps in whose light she would study for school. The sofa was the sofa in whose lap she would grow to adulthood. The mirrors: the mirrors there were backed in silver and framed us in the thick of her house. Yet when we viewed the world inside of them, we did not think *here is this place made silver,* but simply *here is this place:* what does this suggest, we wondered, about the nature of material existence? When I was a small boy, I feared my attic. A ladder depended from a hatch in the hallway, and when my father scaled it into the darkness, I believed, despite the firm white evidence of the ceiling, that he was entering a chamber without a floor. A narrow wooden platform extended into open space, and beneath it lay the deep hidden well of my house: I could see this when I closed my eyes. Though Caroline's house suggested no such fear, it was informed by a similar logic of space: the floors and partitions, the shadows and doorways, were each of them rich with latent dimensions.

It is exactly this sense of latitude and secret depth that my own house is missing. The objects here are only what they are, with nothing to mediate the fact of their existence with the fact of their existence in my life. The walls may be the same hollow blue as a glacier, the carpet as dark as the gravid black sea, and I may be as slight as a boat that skirts the pass, but the walls are only walls, the carpet only carpet, and I am only and ever myself. In the evening, as the sun dwindles to a final red wire at the horizon, I switch on every light and lamp and still my house mushrooms with shadow. I walk from room to room, and everything that belongs to me drifts by like a mist, the wooden shelves banded with book spines, the shoes aligned in the closet, the rounded gray stone that I've carried for years—they are my life's little accidents, a sediment trickled through from my past: they are nothing to do with me. I look, for instance, at the photograph framed on my desk: it sports a slender green tree, a piercing blue sky, and a light that is striking the face that I love. How, I wonder, did I acquire such a thing? It is a gesture of hope simply to open the curtains each morning.

* * *

In truth, I don't know why it ended as it did. When Lewis arrives the next morning, the sun has not yet risen. The sidewalks are starred with mica, and the lawns are sheeted with frost, and the streetlamps glow with a clean white light. He steps to the front porch and presses the doorbell. When the door swings open, it is with such sudden violence that he briefly imagines it has been swallowed, pulled down the gullet of the wide front hall. Thomas Mitchell stands before him wearing striped red nightclothes, his jaw rough with stubble. He has jostled the coatrack on his way to the door, and behind him it sways into the wall, then shudders upright on its wooden paws. He places his hand on the lock plate, thick blue veins roping down his forearm.

"We won't be requiring your services any longer," he says, and his eyebrows shelve together toward his nose, as in a child's drawing of an angry man.

"Pardon?" asks Lewis.

"We don't need you here any more." He announces each syllable of each word, dispassionate and meticulous, as if reciting an oath before a silent courtroom. His body has not moved, only his mouth and eyes.

Lewis would like to ask why, but Thomas Mitchell, taut with bridled anger, stands before him like a dam—exactly that solemn, exactly that impassable—and he decides against it. (*You know why,* the man would say: Lewis can see the words pooled in wait across his features. And yet, though he is coming to understand certain things—that his time here ran to a halt the day before, that his actions then were a form of betrayal—he does not, in fact, know anything.) Instead he asks, "Can I tell her good-bye?" and feels in his stomach a flutter of nervous grief.

"She's not here," says Thomas.

Lisa Mitchell's voice comes questioning from the depths of the house: "What's keeping you?"

Thomas clears his throat. He raises his hand from the lock plate, and his breath comes huffing through his nostrils like a plug of steam. "You can go now," he says, tightening his lips. "I don't expect to see you here again." Then, sliding back into the house, he shuts the door. The bolt engages with a heavy thunk.

Lewis does not know where to go or what to do. He feels like a man who, dashing into the post office to mail a letter, discovers his face on a wanted flier. He stands staring at the doorbell—its orange glow like an ember in a settling fire—until he realizes that he is probably being watched. Glancing at the peephole, he feels the keen electric charge of a hidden gaze. Then he walks across the frost-silvered lawn to his car, his staggered footprints a dark rift in the grass. Lewis drives to the end of the block and parks. He looks into the crux of his steering wheel, his hands tented over his temples, and wonders whether Caroline has been told that he won't be returning.

On the sidewalk, he passes a paperboy who is tossing his folded white missiles from a bicycle; they sail in neat arcs through the air, striking porches and driveways with a leathery slap. He walks around the house to the window of Caroline's bedroom, his heart librating in his chest like a seesaw. The sun will soon rise from behind the curved belly of the fields. The frost will dissipate in the slow heat of morning, and his footprints will dwindle into the green of the lawn.

Caroline is awake in her bed, a sharp light streaming across her face from the open bedroom door. Her pacifier falls from her mouth as she yawns. She wiggles in a pair of fuzzy blue pajamas. Lewis presses himself to the brick of the house and watches her for a few moments. Her body casts a wide shadow over her rumpled yellow bedspread, and it looks as if there is an additional head—his—on the pillow next to hers. He touches his fingers to the window. When he curves and sways them, they look like the spindled legs of an insect. He wants to rap against the glass, to pry it from its frame, to reach across Caroline's blankets and pull her into his arms, but he doesn't.

Instead, he lowers his hand to his side, where it hangs like a plummet on a string, and as a hazy form moves into the glare of the doorway, he turns and retreats to his car. Driving away, he spots a filament of dawn sunlight in the basin of the side-view mirror. He will realize as he slows into his driveway that he has just performed one of the most truly contemptible acts of his life. If he were a good man, he would have found a way, no matter the resistance, to tell her good-bye;

to hand her like an offering some statement of his love; to leave her with at least this much. He could certainly have tried.

He did not, though. He simply left.

* * *

Memories and dreams are the two most potent methods by which the mind investigates itself. Both of them are held by what is not now happening in the world, both of them alert to their own internal motion. I have begun to imagine that they are the same transaction tilted along two separate paths—one into prior possibility, the other into projected. In one of my earliest memories, I am walking through a wooded park with a teacher and my classmates. I carry in my hands a swollen rubber balloon, cherry red and inflated with helium. I don't know where it was purchased, whether it was mine or how long I'd held it, but it was almost as large as the trunk of my body—I remember that. Something jostles me, or my arm grows tired, and I lose my grip. I do not think to reach for the balloon until it has risen into the trees. It floats through a network of leaf-green branches and shrinks in the light of the midday sun. Soon it is only a grain of distant red, and then it vanishes altogether, leaving the blue sky blue and undisturbed.

Remembering this moment, I often dream of Caroline. I dream her resting in my lap and dream her swaying on the swing set. I dream that she is beside me, or I dream that she is approaching. One day, perhaps, we will flee together in my car. We will pass from this town into the rest of our lives, driving through the focus of the narrow black road. On bird-loud summer mornings, as a warm breeze rolls through our windows, we'll watch yellow-green grasshoppers pinging along the verge of the highway. In autumn, the leaves will fall red from the trees as our windshield blades fan away pepperings of rain. The heat will billow from our dashboard vents in winter, and the houses will chimney into the low gray sky. And on the easy, tonic nights of spring, we'll pull to the side of a quiet street and spread ourselves across our ticking hood: we'll watch the far white stars and the soaring red airplanes, ask *Which is the more beautiful? Which is the more true?* and in finding our answers, we will find what we believe in.

Things That Fall from the Sky

It is easier to believe that Yankee professors would lie than that stones would fall from heaven. —Thomas Jefferson, 1803.

Katherine is opening a new book, gluing a lending slip to its blank front page, when she hears the noise again, a clap of sound like the report of a hammer, then another softer clap. This is the third such noise she has heard in ten minutes, and she wonders if she should investigate. "What do you think that noise is?" she asks the other Katherine—Katherine A, people call her. Katherine herself is Katherine B, and there is another Katherine, in Genealogy, who is Katherine C.

"Don't ask me," Katherine A says, staring into the display of her computer monitor. She floats a playing card from one stack to another. "Can't you see that I'm helping a customer?"

This is a game the Katherines play: whoever can tell the most open lie, can hatch the story least in keeping with the truth, gets to idle at the desk while the other sets to work. Katherine A, Katherine concedes, has won the first match.

It is two in the afternoon, a Tuesday, and the library is all but empty. It is quiet and peaceful, and Katherine walks between the rows of books listening to the hum of the air conditioner. Everything drifts around her with a slow, heavy current, and the bookshelves seem to waver and buckle in the silence. She imagines that the light outside the windows is sunlight shifting through water and that she is at the bottom of a deep swimming pool.

At the *Z* end of Bound Periodicals, she finds a man standing at a wooden table, his arms held straight in front of him and a book in either hand. He closes an eye and joggles the books up and down for a moment. Something in his bearing suggests to Katherine a measuring scale—two brass pans hanging from a balance.

She clears her throat. "Excuse me," she says. "May I ask what you're doing?"

"Oh, hello." The man smiles and meets her eye. "It's a test."

"A test?" says Katherine.

"Yes," he says. "A test." He shows her the books. "Gravity's losing."

"I see," says Katherine. Her tone, she hopes, will suggest to him that she doesn't see at all. "Still, if I could ask you to—"

"You've heard that all objects fall at a constant speed. Drop a bowling ball and a marble from the top of a building and they'll hit ground at the same time: that's a law, right? But it's not true," he says.

"Watch." And before she can intercept him, he has squared the books in the air and released them.

The larger book, a hardback, lands on the table with a flat bang, the smaller book an instant later.

Katherine winces. "May I ask you not to do that? There are people trying to read here."

The man looks around at the empty study carrels, at the tables reflecting puddles of light, at the autumn-colored rows of books, and then he laughs, a loud gleeful bark. "What's your name?" he says.

"Katherine B," Katherine answers. Then she feels a prickle of color spreading into her face, something that hasn't happened to her in many years. She corrects herself: "Just Katherine."

"I'm Woodrow," he says. "Just Woodrow. You should read this." He picks up the larger of the two books, the one that landed first, and cocks the spine to display the title: *Things That Fall from the Sky.* "The world is a strange place, Katherine. Did you know that until the nineteenth century, scientists believed that meteorites were just peasant superstition?"

"No, I didn't," she says.

"It's true. I'll have to copy some of this for you." He riffles through the pages of the book.

"Yes, well—" It occurs to Katherine that the man might be out of his mind. Meteorites? Gravity? He is seventy-five or eighty years old, and like her mother he may be showing the first confusions of age. His hair is a pale straw yellow, and the sleeves of his jacket are a cuff or two too long. The skin on his forehead seems to filter into a large central dimple. "If you could just be a little bit quieter," she whispers.

He shrugs his shoulders. "You're the boss," he says. Before she leaves, though, he asks her a question: "Will you be my mother?" he says.

At the desk, Katherine A is still playing solitaire on the computer. She bends closer to the monitor, her face taking on a pallid green glow. Katherine sits heavily beside her and makes a *hmph*ing noise to catch her attention. "I just met a crazy man," she says.

Katherine A looks at her and gives a needle-thin sigh. "This is a *library*," she says. "There's nothing *but* crazy men. What do you want, a cookie?"

* * *

That evening, Katherine finds a message from her son Peter on the answering machine. Peter is the younger of her two boys—a happy, noisy, eager-hearted child who somehow became, when she wasn't looking, a lonely, sullen man. He manages a drugstore now in London, and though he calls once a month, she suspects that he no longer loves her. After he moved, she discovered a half-written letter in his bedroom, addressed to his older brother, that pierced her heart like a baited trap. "You're lucky to be living your life," it read. "I want no more of this place—no family, no home, no quiet little town. It's only holding me back. Sometimes I think that even an ocean won't be far enough."

She gazes at the blinking red message light and listens to his voice on the answering machine; it speaks quickly lest she should arrive home unexpectedly. "Hey, Mom, this is Peter, just calling to touch base. It's eight o'clock here, and you're probably still at work. Everything's fine, it's raining outside, things are busy at the store. You know how it is. Give me a call sometime."

Katherine lets his phone ring eleven times before she hangs up.

Later that night, after she has eaten dinner, she calls her other son,

Tanner, who lives across town with his wife and daughter. Tanner is on the creative development team for a national breakfast food manufacturer and is trying to find a name for a new product. "It's a tropical fruit–flavored cereal," he tells her. "Little pineapples and bananas and coconuts. What do you think of 'Fruit Island Cereal'?"

"That sounds familiar," she says. "Wasn't there a Fruit Island something a few years ago?"

"Familiar is good. People will think it's an old favorite."

"Still," she hesitates. "How about 'Tropical-Ohs'?"

"Mom." Tanner squeezes the word from his mouth like an egg. "I don't try to explain the Dewey Decimal System to *you,* do I? Besides, they're fruit-shaped, not O-shaped."

Katherine changes the subject. "Have you talked to Peter lately? He phoned today and sounded depressed on the machine." She thinks of her son and a sadness moves through her. "Oh, Tanner, does he let anyone know him at all? Is it just me? I feel like I haven't heard his voice in years."

Tanner hesitates for a moment, then says, "Fruity Yum-Yums."

A ripple of sound comes over the line. It is his daughter Robin, Katherine's granddaughter, four years old and full of joy and commotion. She is not yet lost to the world, and Katherine treasures her.

"Robin says hi," Tanner tells her.

"Let me talk to her. Put her on."

There is a muffled seashell emptiness on the line and Katherine knows that he has pressed the receiver to his chest, something he used to do when he was living at home. She hears him saying quietly, "Grandma says hi, too," and then the air parts around his voice. "It's her bedtime, Mom, I don't want to get her all excited. Tell you what: this weekend you can take her out for ice cream. How does that sound?"

"Fine," says Katherine. "It's a date," she says.

"Good," says Tanner. "I've got to go now, Mom. Take care." He hangs up before she can say good-bye.

The next day, Katherine is leaving the library for lunch, rummaging for her car keys in the jumbled nest of her purse, when she discovers a slip of paper on her windshield. It is battened under a wiper blade, and a loose upper corner of it shudders in the breeze. At first she thinks that it's a promotional leaflet or a parking ticket, but when she pulls it free she sees that it is covered to the margins with a dense, weblike handwriting.

In April of 1987, the Rev. John Cotton of Chester, England, witnessed a fall of "hundreds of fishes" during a late afternoon thunderstorm. He gathered several and placed them in his bathtub, but they died before he could secure them food, from which he determined that they were a saltwater breed. All were about two inches in length. A local angler identified them as small stickleback. ★ Portland, Oregon. 1974. Ms. Cora Block heard something on the roof of her house that, she said, "sounded like hail." When she went outside to investigate, she found that her front yard and roof were both covered with live frogs. At first she thought that somebody was playing a practical joke on her, but she could see nobody in the area. The last few frogs fell as she was watching. The sky was clear. ★ Reported in the journal L'Astronomie, 1890, p. 272: A stone of unknown origin, which geologists were unable to identify, fell to earth in 1872 near the town of Banjite, Servia. It was unlike any stone that scientists had theretofore catalogued, and they designated it with the name Banjite. Another stone of Banjite fell in Servia in 1876, and another in 1889. Nowhere else have such stones been found. ★ In February of 1996, John Young of Bloomington, Indiana, was struck on the foot by a six-inch metal rod, an inch in diameter, while working in his garden. He was wearing heavy leather dock boots at the time, but the rod still broke two of his metatarsals, which demanded surgery. He described the rod as "burning hot" and said that it displayed shear marks at both its ends. The Bloomington Regional Airport reported no planes in the area at the time of this incident. Mr. Young speculated that "some sort of catapult or sling" was involved. ★ In the Deipnosophistae of Athenaeus, written in Greece in 200 A.D., there is a chapter entitled "De pluvius piscium." This chapter tells of a rain of fish in Chersonesus that continued for three days. Athenaeus writes that "certain persons have in many places seen it rain fishes, and the same thing often happens with tadpoles." ★ In 1990, while boating on a lake with some friends, Claire Mooney of Springfield, Missouri, was caught in a downpour of onion bulbs. They fell, she said, for about twenty seconds, and only in the immediate vicinity of her vessel. Her companions verified this story to the Springfield Clarion-Ledger, stating that one of the bulbs hit Ms. Mooney in the eye, scratching her retina. "I shouldn't have looked up," she told reporters. ★ In Calabria, Italy, in May of 1890, a substance the color and consistency of fresh blood fell from the sky. Similar falls had been reported in the region in 1814 and 1860. Scientists who examined the substance found that it was corpuscular in nature. They claimed that it was birds' blood, though no feathers or other such material was found. Cosmographer Charles Fort, who relates this incident in The Book of the Damned, speculates "that something far from this earth had bled, that there are oceans of blood, somewhere in the sky."

Katherine finishes reading the slip of paper—a letter, should she call it?—and looks around for the man she met the day before. He is nowhere to be found, but she is certain that the letter is his, and this unnerves her. Where is he now? She steps into her car, starts the engine, and pulls out of the library parking lot. As she drives away, he seems to rise up before her in every face she sees, floating through them one by one like a thread drawn through an eyelet: through the teacher standing in the school yard, through the businessman hailing a taxi, through the traffic cop standing on the highway safety island, through the GOOD CHRISTIAN MAN who WILL WORK FOR FOOD.

It is Friday morning and Katherine is hosting a tour of the library for a group of junior high school students. She is leading them past the map room and the state document archives, explaining in what she hopes is her least stuffy voice that they should not think of libraries as mausoleums or petrified forests, as stacks of old books with fossil ideas, but that libraries can be living places, that every book there can be like a person, and a person who truly wants to be known, she tells them, a person who will give you the best of himself if not the whole of himself, and where else can you find *that*?

The students are following along behind her like a carnival parade.

A boy with tinted black glasses and a downy mustache is kissing his girlfriend with a piglike rooting noise. Another boy is flexing a steel ruler in his hands and snapping it across the butt of the girl in front of him. A cheerleader in a black-and-gold uniform is pulling books from the shelves at random, fanning the pages into her face and idly inhaling the scent. The escort for the field trip, a moon-faced woman whom the children call Miss Grandon, is paying no attention to them whatsoever: she keeps sniffling and dabbing at the edge of her eye with a tissue. When Katherine presses her own eye in imitation, a dark spot, like a splash of ink, appears in the opposite corner.

At the end of the tour, as they congregate around the front desk, Katherine asks the children if they have any questions for her.

A girl raises her hand. "Whatever happened to the Bookmobile?"

The Bookmobile was a converted school bus, bookstacks housed around the ribbed central aisle, that used to carry best-sellers and picture books to the shopping plazas around town. "It still runs," answers Katherine. "But we didn't have the money to keep the full route going. It travels by appointment now, mostly to churches and nursery schools." She turns again to the crowd. "Any other questions?"

A boy in a canvas army jacket asks her, "Where do you keep the pornography?" and is greeted with a chop or two of stifled laughter from his friends.

The class escort, Miss Grandon, clears her throat, and her body seems to tighten in on itself. "That's enough, *Eric,*" she says, accenting his name at both syllables.

"No, it's okay," says Katherine. She answers this question several times a week and considers it standard information, like where to find the restrooms or how to position a book on the Xerox machine. "We carry art and photography on the west side of the second floor, but you're probably looking for the glossy magazines. Those are behind the Periodicals desk, in the closed stacks, but you have to be eighteen before we'll retrieve them for you."

The boy in the army jacket looks surprised by her answer, or by the fact that she answered at all. His mouth is twisting into a strange shape. Miss Grandon gives an indignant *hrrum* and takes the girl standing next to her by the wrist. "We're leaving, kids," she says. Her face is firm and bloodless. "*Now.*"

The children begin to talk to one another in a flurry of murmurs and whispers, adjusting their bookbags and peeking at Katherine from behind the collars of their jackets. She watches them flow through the double glass doors into the sunlight.

Katherine A is sitting at the front desk, shaking her head. "What on earth did you do that for?" she asks.

"What?" says Katherine. With her thumbs she taps a little tattoo on the desk.

Katherine A shakes her head again. "That teacher didn't look too happy. Notice that?"

She did notice, of course, and it comes to her like a light that the teacher was unhappy with *her,* not the boy. For the second time in a week she feels her face coloring with heat.

Outside, the children have all filed onto the school bus, and Katherine looks up to see Miss Grandon glaring at her from behind the door. She storms back inside, her walk full of anger and purpose, swinging a heavy gray purse at her side like a horseshoe or a bowling ball. Katherine imagines for a moment that she is going to strike her with it, but instead she stops at Katherine's breast and drops the purse at her feet.

"I apologize," says Katherine, preempting Miss Grandon as the woman takes a breath. "I'm sorry. I wasn't thinking."

What she means to say—what she is, in fact, thinking—is this: *I don't know what's become of me or who I'm supposed to be. My sense of what it takes to live with other people is slowly drifting away. My thoughts have become a mystery to me. I watch myself speaking lately and it's as if I were somewhere else. It's as if my life were being displayed before me on a table: I could carry it off in my hand, place it in a box or a drawer, and forget that it was even there. More and more I think as I grow older that I live in this world and know nothing about it.*

"Damn right you weren't." Miss Grandon pokes her finger at Katherine's ribs as she talks but doesn't actually touch her, so that the gesture seems strangely weightless. "Don't think for a second that I won't report this," she says, and when Katherine doesn't respond, she adds, "because I will."

"I get so used to answering questions," Katherine says.

"To kids? About pornography? I can tell you this," Miss Grandon says. "When somebody's parents go crying to the school board that little Johnny Thompson learned about skin magazines at the library today, it won't be my ass on the line."

Katherine hesitates for a moment, not sure she should continue. "They just seemed like people," she says quietly. "I thought I could treat them like regular people."

"In junior high?" Miss Grandon picks up her purse. "Lady, we can't even teach *Huckleberry Finn* to these kids."

She heads for the doorway, but stops before she reaches it. "*You* screwed up," she says, "*not* me. I'm not the bad influence here."

Then she swivels on the balls of her feet and is gone.

The bus pulls away in a blur of yellow. Katherine takes a seat behind the desk.

"You'll have to excuse me for a second," says Katherine A, standing. A laugh is sneaking into the corners of her mouth, and as her hand finds the door to the bathroom it escapes in a sudden snort.

Katherine rests her head on the desk, hooking her fingers around the edge of the raised front counter. She closes her eyes and small twists of color swim across the darkness. They look, these designs, like Chinese ideograms, like messages from some foreign language, and she wishes that she could decipher them. Should she have stopped herself from answering the boy in the army jacket? She doesn't know. But there is a little knot of worry in her stomach suggesting that she should have.

She feels the touch of another hand against her own and when she lifts her head, she sees the man who was dropping books the other day behind Bound Periodicals. "I was watching earlier," he says. "You didn't do anything wrong. You should know that."

Though she suspects she should be alarmed that this man is touching her, there is something calming in the pressure of his hand. It draws whatever fear she might feel away, sending it into the sky, in spite of which she says, "I'm not your mother."

He gives a slow, thinking smile. "Okay."

"Did you put a note on my windshield?"

"Of course." He places his other hand on the counter. "But about those kids: this is what I wanted to say: you're not a bad person—that woman was wrong. You simply confused them. Sometimes people don't really want the answers they ask for. What they want is a reflex response—a laugh or a look of sympathy, even a punch in the face. They want to be recognized," he says. "We're all built that way, I'm afraid."

Katherine doesn't know what to say. These are kind words, the most compassionate she has heard in a long time, and she is taken aback that they have come from the mouth of this man.

"Thank you," she begins, and then realizes that she doesn't remember his name. "I'm sorry, I—"

"Woodrow," he says. He retrieves his hand from atop her own and gives her a brisk salute good-bye.

As he leaves, she repeats his name: "Woodrow."

Even after the sun has risen, Katherine lies in bed simply listening to the world for a time. She hears a squirrel chiseling at a nut outside her window. She hears the knocking of tennis shoes along the sidewalk. Her breathing is peaceful and steady, and her blood tingles warmly in her hands and feet. As she rests there, her bedroom seems to widen with light, and the quiet, steady motion of it makes her think of golden fields of grass, drifting in long waves in the breeze. It is Saturday.

Katherine has promised to take her granddaughter Robin out for ice cream, and after she has showered and dressed, she drives across town to Tanner's house, skirting the edge of Lake Sodowsky to avoid traffic. When she reaches Chestnut Street, the neighborhood children are playing a game of street hockey with a tennis ball. They part before her car in that resolute, mannish way of boys pretending to be athletes.

She coasts to a stop beside Tanner's mailbox. His car is parked in his driveway, and his yard has been freshly mowed. Her feet kick up loose shocks of grass as she walks to the door.

She can hear voices coming from inside the house. "What did I tell you?" her son shouts. Ever since he was a boy he has suffered from fits of improbable anger—fits that would seize him for a few minutes and then just boil away—but this is the first time Katherine has heard him in such a temper in his own home. "Your grandmother will be here any minute. Put the damn puzzle up and get your shoes on!"

Robin says something that Katherine cannot quite make out. Her words are halting and breathy, like a breeze coming through the joints of a window.

"Don't talk back to me!" Tanner shouts.

There is a sudden light pattering noise—puzzle pieces falling to the carpet, Katherine thinks—and then the slap of skin against skin. Robin starts to cry.

Katherine feels a rising heat in her chest and she raps on the door.

"Just a minute!" calls Tanner.

When he appears in the doorway, he has composed himself. "Mom!" he says, registering excitement in his voice. "Come on in. Robin will be ready in just a minute." He turns to his daughter, who is standing behind him and snuffling back tears. "Go get your shoes on, honey," he says gently.

Robin rushes past, and Katherine sees a mottled red handprint on her bare leg. She steps inside, shuts the door, and looks her son in the eye. *"Tanner,"* she admonishes him.

"What?" he says. *"What?"*

"She's just a child."

His face grows hard. "With all due respect, Mom," he says, "you know nothing about it. It's been fifteen years since you were a parent: your time has passed you by."

Katherine doesn't know what to say to this. "Your father and I never struck you, Tanner. Not once."

"*You* never struck me," Tanner says. "Dad did, sometimes, when I got out of line, and it did me a world of good."

Katherine is taken aback. Her ex-husband, who now lives in Minneapolis with his second wife, has struck her son—this is a new fact. "I . . ." she says. "I didn't know that." She wonders if she should place a hand on his arm, but she can see him flinching away from her.

"You didn't need to," he says.

Robin runs up the hall from her bedroom, wearing clean white socks and sandals made of sparkly pink rubber. Though her cheeks are still wet, she is no longer crying. "I'm ready," she says, and she takes Katherine's hand.

Tanner escorts them onto the porch. "You two have a good time," he says. Their conversation is at an end.

In the car, while Katherine shudders onto an access road over a set of rumble strips, Robin tells her that she would rather eat at her favorite restaurant, KidBurgers, than at the ice cream parlor. In her high, flat-toned singing voice, she delivers the first few lines of the

KidBurgers jingle: *KidBurgers / KidBurgers / The burger place for kids! / A toy with every meal! / What a deal!*

"Did your father come up with a name for his cereal?" Katherine asks.

"No," says Robin. "He's been walking around the house testing names for a week."

At the restaurant, Robin orders a cheeseburger, fries, and a strawberry milkshake, Katherine a chicken sandwich and a diet cola. The boy behind the counter hands their food to them inside a checkered cardboard KidBurgers tray, along with a box of four wax crayons. Robin pours salt and pepper directly into her ketchup thimble, stirring them into the sauce with her fries, a habit she learned from her father, who learned it long ago from his own. "Do you want to hear what happened in school last week?" she says. "I won the Most Enthusiastic Student award." She tells Katherine that she got to be the line leader when they went to the playground, and that she bounced on a trampoline in gymnastics after lunch one day, and that a boy named Jason lodged an apple seed in his ear on Friday and had to leave before TV time to go to the doctor. Katherine nods, only half listening, and takes a sip of her soda. The sun is shining onto their table through the window, and birds are flailing about in the sky.

"Tell me," she asks. "How often does your dad get mad at you?"

"Not very. He yells sometimes. Mom says it's his *job* that does the yelling, not him."

There are times, Katherine thinks, when her granddaughter seems to have the grace and poise and self-possession of a full-grown woman, like a coin sent whirling for a moment on its edge. "Did he get mad at you before I came over today?"

Robin signals with her finger to wait a second, sucking a globule of shake through her straw. She swallows, takes another sip, and swallows again. "No," she finally says.

When they have finished their lunch, Katherine drives Robin to the grocery store. "I'll buy you a coloring book to go with your crayons," she says, and Robin begins to shift about excitedly, zipping her thumbnail back and forth over her seat belt.

Katherine has always found grocery stores strangely reassuring. Shopping carts with rattling silver baskets. Automatic doors with pressure-sensitive exit pads. Weighing scales and cheese displays and mounds of shining fruit. The people in grocery stores know what they're there for, lists of things to purchase gripped in their hands. They wheel from aisle to aisle, gradually filling their baskets, passing each other like ducks on a pond and converging finally at the cash registers. Also, there is the basic grocery store floor plan, a single, universal design that she has found to be the standard—vegetables at one end and dairy products at the other, meats along the back wall and frozen foods down the center aisle. She takes comfort in this lack of surprise.

After they have parked, Robin leads Katherine straight to the breakfast foods section, stopping at a rack of cheap toys and magazines and sifting through the coloring books. "I think I want this one," Robin says, examining her options. She holds up a coloring book with the title *Ponies and Princesses* on the cover, her hand obscuring a picture of a unicorn.

Katherine hears a voice behind her say, "Hello."

When she turns to look, it is the man from the library. "Where did you come from?" she asks. This is the first time she has seen him outside the library, and she wonders if perhaps he has been following her.

"Just purchasing a few necessities," he says. He grins as he talks, his head bobbing idly on his neck. "Loaf of bread"—he displays in his left hand a loaf of bread—"and carton of eggs"—he jiggles a carton of eggs in his other.

Robin is watching him with undisguised curiosity, clearly not at all wary. She is enjoying this strange glimpse into her grandmother's life. "Hi," she tells the man. "I'm Robin."

"Robin," he answers, "I'm pleased to make your acquaintance. My name is Woodrow." He stoops to his knees and meets her face to face. "And I think your mom is the *best* mom in the *whole* world."

"Grandmom, actually," says Katherine—though why she feels the need to clarify this, she doesn't know.

"We had cheeseburgers for lunch," says Robin.

"*Cheese*burgers!" exclaims Woodrow. His eyes bug out and he laughs as if she has just told a tremendous joke. "You don't make *burgers* out of *cheese*!"

Robin giggles. "Yes, you do!" she says. "And then we came here for a coloring book, because I got crayons with my cheeseburger. See, I'll show you." She shakes the crayons from her crayon box onto her palm. "Blue, yellow, orange, and green."

"Mm-hm," Woodrow says. "Four crayons. So where did you leave your mommy, Robin? I hope you didn't lose her."

"She stayed home with Daddy."

"This little piggie went to market," he says, tapping her on the nose, "and that little piggie stayed home."

Robin smiles. "Which little piggie are you?"

Woodrow gives a theatrical scratch to his chin, thinks for a moment, and then appears to experience a great revelation. He stands and his knees crack. "Whee, whee, whee!" he cries. He trots to the end of the aisle, disappearing around the bend. His voice stops abruptly—for a moment it seems that he has simply dissolved away—but then his head appears from around the corner and he waves good-bye.

When it becomes clear that he is not going to return, Katherine takes her granddaughter by the shoulder and asks her if she is ready to go. Robin is clutching her coloring book in a rolled-up tube, staring up the aisle as if a train has just departed there.

"Where did he go?" she says.

Katherine makes a wide, stumped gesture with her arms. "I have no idea," she says.

Robin thinks for a moment. A pale fluorescent light flickers overhead, and a shopping cart with an unpinned wheel jerks past. "I *like* him," she finally says.

On Sunday Katherine visits her mother at the Briarwood Nursing Facility, a converted hotel in the center of the downtown business district. She is lying in her bedroom, her head propped crookedly on a pillow, and a flower pot is tucked beneath her arm. Katherine can see that this is one of her bad days. She seats herself on the edge of the bed and leans over, placing a kiss on her mother's forehead. There is a fog of misunderstanding in her eyes.

"Mom," Katherine says, smoothing the skin of her hand. "Mom, do you recognize me?"

"Hello, dear," her mother says. Then adds, after a moment, "Katherine."

"How have you been?" Katherine asks. "Have you been sleeping well?"

"Look at that giant woman," her mother says. She gestures weakly toward the window, which presents to her room a view of a billboard. Giant woman? The model in the advertisement holds a long brown cigarette in the crook of her fingers. The left half of her body has come unglued, stripped from the billboard like bark from a birch tree. It hangs past the walkway and twists loosely in the high breeze, and in the opening it leaves Katherine can see the face and arm of another woman, larger than the first, fingering the stem of a cocktail glass.

"She's splitting in two," says her mother, "but she's still laughing. Why do you think she's still laughing? Do you suppose it tickles to have her in there?"

Katherine guesses that the "her" her mother is referring to is the second woman, the one inside the other.

"I wish you had a better view, Mom. Have you asked the nurses about being moved to the other side of the building?"

Her mother does not answer.

"I can talk to someone for you if you'd like."

She closes her eyes, her plum-colored eyelids shivering once or twice behind thick spectacles.

Katherine has just begun to think that she has fallen asleep—lately her mother seems to drop away instantaneously—when suddenly she breaks the silence. "Tell that boy to visit," she says. Her eyes are still shut. "Tanner. That son of yours. I'd like to see my great grand-"—her voice fades away for a moment and she opens her eyes—"daughter."

"I'll do that."

A man with an aluminum walker scuffs by in the hallway, and a car horn sounds on the street. There is an air of stillness and exhaustion in the building, a forgetfulness in the faces of the nurses and residents. It is as if the days and months and even the seasons here are without aim or effect or intelligibility.

"Let me tell you about my week," says Katherine. "I took Robin to lunch yesterday. We ate at KidBurgers. Did you know that she dips her french fries just like Tanner does? *He* learned it from *his* dad, and *she* learned it from him. It made me think of all the things I've learned from you, all the little habits and mannerisms. I still carry extra buttons in my wallet, did you know that? Just like you always did. I still eat my meals one ingredient at a time and I still wait for the third ring before I answer the phone. That's what makes us family, I think—little things like that . . . What else happened this week? I met a man at work—"

"He always leaves that there," her mother says, grimacing.

"Pardon?"

Her mother looks toward the doorway, and Katherine turns to see a metal carriage there, weighted down with blankets. "Would you be a dear and move that for me?" her mother asks.

"Of course," says Katherine. "On my way out."

"Good," her mother says, and yawns. "I had a dream about your father last night. I wanted to tell you that. We were living in our first house, the house we bought when he got his promotion. The one with the deck in the back and the pine trees in the yard. You were just a baby. Do you remember that? It was summer and—oh—something happened. It was a lovely dream. We were very, very happy." She sighs. "Why doesn't your father ever come to see me? Have you asked him why he never comes to see me?"

Katherine feels a prickle of fear—almost panic—washing through her. She can feel it in her hands and in her shoulders. Her father is seven years dead now, resting beneath a tablet in the Edgewood Memorial Cemetery, and this is the first time her mother has forgotten his loss, the first time she has restored him to life in her mind. Carefully, Katherine says, "Mom, Dad passed on. Don't you remember? He had a heart attack and died in the hospital."

Her mother's mouth gives a sudden tic at the corner, and her eyes grow misty with tears. Katherine can see the realization washing through her: he has left her behind and she is all alone in the world.

Katherine leans over her mother's bed to embrace her, resting her arms against the stiff white sheets. "Oh, Mom," she says. And then, against her cheek, she feels a sudden hard slap.

She draws back, startled.

Her mother's hand is raised, her face braided with anger. "Don't you *ever* talk about your father that way!" she says.

The next day, at the library, Katherine finds herself hoping that Woodrow will reappear. She listens for the rasp of his old man's voice, the fall of his shoes in the aisle, the clapping of books against a wooden table. She volunteers to shelve the titles in the returns cart, taking frequent walks around the library. When he doesn't appear, she feels curiously disappointed.

"Have you ever heard of strange objects falling from the sky?" she asks Katherine A.

"What, like meteors?"

"Meteors," says Katherine, "or fish, or frogs, or blood."

Katherine A considers for a moment. "I was struck on the head once by a nut," she says. "I was standing under a chestnut tree."

"No," says Katherine. "You know what I mean."

"I heard this rumble while I was in bed last night. When I looked outside, *water* was falling from the sky." Katherine A is clearly enjoying herself. "Nails and shingles fall from construction sites. Birds fall when they're shot by bullets. The devil is supposed to be a fallen angel. Oh, and then there's the Fall of Man—"

"Never mind," says Katherine.

That afternoon, shortly before she is scheduled to go home, she receives a letter from the director of Library Services: *It has come to my attention that you have been engaging in lewd discussions with minors visiting our facility. Contact my office ASAP so that we may discuss this matter further.* It's signed: *Most sincerely, Dick Ridling, Director of Library Services.*

"Did you know about this?" she asks Katherine A.

"Let me see." She reads the letter and hands it back, giving a little puff of indifference. "News to me," she says. "But I can't say I'm bowled over by it."

"Great," Katherine sighs. "Perfect." She slips the letter into her purse, then stands and pulls her jacket from the back of her chair. "I'll see you tomorrow," she says.

"Tomorrow," says Katherine A.

Though a mass of gray clouds is rolling in from the west, little bubbles of sunlight are still glinting from the hoods of the cars in the parking lot. Katherine is parked beneath a thick black walnut tree. When she steps around its buttress of roots, she finds another slip of paper on her windshield. *Woodrow,* she thinks, and she fills first with a sense of relief, then with a sense of surprise at her relief. She opens the flier and reads:

Annual Red Cross Blood Drive
October 2–8
At the Fletcher County Hospital

Beneath this is an illustration of a smiling red blood drop holding a yardstick, followed by the line:

Every Drop Counts!

When she looks around, she sees these squares of paper beneath the blades of every car in the parking lot, like rows of white headstones in a cemetery. Katherine has never been comfortable with needles; in fact, they terrify her. She folds the leaflet in half, tosses it toward the open lid of a trash basket, and watches as it goes maple-leafing to the ground.

At home, there is another message from her son waiting for her on the answering machine: "Hey, Mom. Peter again. You're probably working, so we'll talk some other time. I'll be busy for a few days, so don't bother to call. Bye." She erases the message as she slips from her shoes, then drops wearily onto the bed and closes her eyes. She listens to the arms of the ceiling fan splitting the air—*whup, whup, whup.* After a few minutes she rises and walks to the window. The weather has broken and it is showering outside, fine particles of rain that she can only detect because of a slight tapping motion in the leaves. The relaxation in the air and the slow darkening of the room calls up a spell of old recollections. She remembers, all at once, many things, and these things seem both free-floating and particular, clear and disconnected, as if the strings between them have come unfastened. She remembers biting the inside of her cheek when she was a little girl: she was stepping onto a school bus, and the thin taste of blood in her mouth was buttery and familiar. She remembers counting to seven and jumping from a staircase, the tingle in her feet when she hit the floor. She remembers her grandmother calling her "my little drop of sunlight." She remembers kissing her college boyfriend on a spring day, squeezing his knee by the fountain in back of the student union. She remembers the black chocolate cake she made for her mother's sixtieth birthday, Tanner and Peter chasing each other with plastic swords, the chop of water against a boat pier. She remembers yellow leaves falling in an autumn wind. She remembers her house on Christmas morning. She remembers her husband boxing his books away and her children leaving for college and her dad in white sheets in a hospital bed. She remembers these things as if no one memory is connected to any other—as if each makes known a different place and life, a thousand different places and a thousand different lives. She presses her forehead to the glass and looks outside, wondering how all these many places came to be this one room and this one window, how all these many people came to be just her, her alone, the woman who wouldn't give her blood away.

And so, on Tuesday, though Katherine is sitting before a mahogany desk in the office of Mr. Ridling, and though he is dressing her down for her lack of good judgment, she does not hesitate to leave when the moment arrives.

"So what do you propose we do about this?" Mr. Ridling is saying. "I know that from your perspective it might seem somewhat *unorthodox* to suggest such a thing—that we should reserve certain materials for our patrons who are, shall we say, *of age*—but then again, we can't have our librarians just blithely violating the basic rules of polite society, now can we?"

That's when Katherine hears the sound: the double *bang* of falling books. She stands to leave.

"Where do you think you're going?" says Mr. Ridling.

She hesitates in the doorway, her hand on the brushed metal knob. Mr. Ridling is tapping at his desk. "I'll be right back," Katherine says.

The library is quiet and still, and the sunlight shimmers through the high windows. As she walks from room to room, Katherine can hear her footsteps echoing softly against the walls of shelving. She listens to herself tapping along. Woodrow is not in Fiction, where she expected him to be, and he is not in Bound Periodicals. He is not in the Music Lab or the Map Room, the Reference Stacks or the Children's Collection. He is not in Genealogy.

She finds him instead at a table in the rear corner of New Acquisitions, weighing a book in either hand.

"Hello," she says.

"Oh, hi," he answers. He is wearing the same oversized jacket as before, his hair the same straw yellow, his eyes the same pale blue. He shows her the books. "One more test. Just to make sure."

Katherine reaches for the books. "Allow me?" she asks.

Woodrow seems surprised. His eyebrows arch, which makes the dimple in the center of his forehead wink shut like an eye. "Of course," he says.

She takes the books from his hands, weighs them for a second in her own, and then drops them squarely onto the wooden table, where they land in sequence, one following the other, *bang bang.* "Now," she says. She brushes her hands together. "How would you like to go to lunch? We'll just walk outside—that's what we'll do—and I'll take you to lunch."

His face registers genuine pleasure. "I'd like that, Katherine."

"Good," she says. She takes him by the arm and leads him down the aisle.

Apples

The fall of my thirteenth year was a time when all the important events in my life seemed to cluster together like bees. On the same sun-bright afternoon that I won the school spelling bee, my parents sat across from me in the living room and told me that they no longer loved each other, and a great gray ocean of wishlessness filled our house. Days like this would surface around me every few weeks: I was chased to my front door by a stray dog on the same day that I had my braces removed. I answered the phone to an obscene caller on the same night that my mom went to live with a stranger. And on the same November day that I received my first kiss from Allison Downey, I watched my Bible teacher, Coach Schramm, get killed by a bucket. This took place at the Heritage Christian Academy, a private junior high school run by the Church of Christ. We assembled there each morning in the chapel for a prayer, rode our buses home each afternoon across the river, and gathered in between to study grammar and human fitness, biology and the King James Scriptures.

On the morning of his last autumn storm, Coach Schramm walked between the chalkboard and his desk, tapping at his leg with an index rod as he told us about the Creation. I remember that I was tracing a line of graffiti in my desktop, a pair of capital U's channeled with the scorings of many pencils and pens. Thunder was grumbling from a fish-white sky, and there was a bias and stress to the air that made the sounds of the classroom seem bold and sudden, like voices speaking out of a long silence. A wristwatch beeped the hour. Lead ticked from a mechanical pencil. After two weeks of nothing, I could feel my life assembling inside itself a certain urgency.

Coach Schramm stood for a moment at the chalkboard, tall and ropy in his shirt and tie. His sleeves were gathered at the elbows, and the lanyard of a whistle dangled from his breast pocket. "And on the sixth day, God created—what?" he asked.

Nobody answered. Jeff Cypert dropped his notebook. Max Krain gave an emphatic sniffle.

"The beasts of the earth and man in his image," he said, and then he repeated himself, stressing the cardinal words: the *beasts* of the *earth* and *man* in his *image.* "Come on, folks," he continued. "Eyes on the ball."

We had begun the year with Lamentations and Ezekiel, but were returning to Genesis as a preface to Daniel. "A warm-up," Coach Schramm had announced, twirling his whistle around his finger. He taught volleyball, the Old Testament, and track and field, and he had introduced himself in August as our Bible Coach. When we lingered over a test or pop quiz, he would clap his hands and tell us to hustle.

Coach Schramm opened his Bible, leafing past the maps and the foreword, and I watched, as I always did, each thin translucent page catch the air and hover for a moment before it fell. He read, "And God made the beast of the earth after his kind, and cattle after their kind, and every thing that creepeth upon the earth after his kind: and God saw that it was good." This had been our memory verse earlier in the semester, and hearing it again after so many weeks was peculiar, like discovering that a twist of metal you'd been carrying in your pocket was part of some intricate machine.

Coach Schramm spread the Bible open on his desk and placed a stick of chalk in the valley. "So that's the sixth day. Who can remind us what happened on the third? Mister Bozeman?"

Walter Bozeman turned from the window, where a pitch pine was slanting back and forth in the wind. He blinked at his notebook paper and his voice gave a little skip. "The moon and the stars?" he said.

"That's day four, Walt. Who can take the ball on this one? Mister Cave?"

"Trees and dry land, Coach."

"Good." Coach Schramm cupped one hand around the other and cracked his knuckles. Outside, it began to rain. "And the fifth day?"

Dewey Nichols, who sat beside me, tilted forward in his desk.

"Yes, Mister Nichols?"

Dewey cleared his throat. "The birds and the fish. But I have a question: the pattern seems to be that God creates something, then sees that it's good. But on the second day, when he splits the world in two, it doesn't happen that way. He divides the heavens from the seas, and then that's it. He just moves on. Why?"

Coach Schramm was pacing the room. "I don't know," he said, "what do you think, Dewey?" and Dewey gave his familiar reply: "I don't know, either, but I think it bears looking into."

Jason Cooley asked, "Now *when* did God create the waters?" and Coach said, "Chapter one, verse two: and the spirit of God moved upon the face of the waters." Kyle Hoftyzer asked whether "male and female created he them" meant both Adam *and* Eve, and Coach said that it meant first Adam, then Eve. Jeff Cypert asked when our next test would be, and Coach said he would let us know.

Then Ryan Biggum raised his hand and asked about the dinosaurs. "Where do *they* fit in?" he said. I had known Ryan Biggum for eight years, and in that time he had questioned every adult in our school on this matter—every teacher, every parent, every visiting speaker. He was dissatisfied with the suggestion that the dinosaurs had perished in the Flood, and he frequently said, in class, that he considered their absence "a hole too big to fit through." Ryan Biggum was a mess.

"I've done some searching," he continued, "and as far as I can tell they're not mentioned *anywhere.*"

Standing at the window Coach Schramm looked as shadowy and grave as any ancient pharaoh. He sighed in a way that seemed to suggest he'd taught a few too many Ryan Biggums in his time. "God Almighty," he said, rainwater battering against the glass all around him. "Can't we give the dinosaurs a rest?"

My school building stood on a bluff overlooking the river and the highway, and its western face was as much window as brick. Wide bands of glass stretched from the roof to the ground—on those evenings when my father drove me to football games or drama productions, they shone in the light of the sun like open doorways—and a window cleaner's scaffold hung from a derrick at the fourth floor. It was this scaffold that ruptured in the wind that day, releasing a coiled hose, a washrag, and a metal bucket secured to a guy rope—and it was this bucket that lifted like a jackstone into the storm, shot to the end of its rope, and as Coach Schramm sighed his displeasure, came spinning down into the side of our building. It shattered through our schoolroom window—I thought for a moment that I was listening to the dumpster lid slamming open outside. Then it struck Coach Schramm on the spine of his nose and went swinging back into the rain.

Of course, none of us knew that the scaffold had split, or the bucket had toppled, or the rope had turned at the time. We knew only this: that Coach Schramm had taken the Lord's name in vain, then fallen in a cataract of breaking glass.

He landed with an awful crack, his whistle clattering to the floor beside him.

For a moment, everything was silent. A yellow maple leaf blew in through the window, and the bucket flashed back and forth there like a bob weight.

Though his lip showed only the barest splash of blood, Coach Schramm was not moving.

The ceiling vent began to whisper with warm air.

"Someone should probably go tell the office," I said.

Robert Shriver dropped his pencil.

Max Krain sneezed like a cannon.

My fourth-period English teacher, Mister Schramm, was an open, gregarious man who was quite popular in our school. He hosted field trips to plays and museums, recited stories with a performer's voice, and wore neckties with prints of woodland animals on them. He was Coach Schramm's younger brother. Earlier in the week, he had announced that we would compete as teams that day in a vocabulary contest. Instead we arrived in class to find him staring up at the mercury light, his eyeglasses propped on his forehead, his necktie draped across the corner of his desk. A note was waiting for us on the chalkboard: "Pick up worksheets from podium. Study quietly for preposition exam."

For fifty-five minutes, until it was time for lunch, Mister Schramm sat at the front of the classroom running his thumb down the tines of a plastic comb. It sounded like the throating of frogs in a creekbed.

"So where did they take him?" asked Lelah Holeman, twisting the cap off a chocolate sandwich cookie.

The lunchroom was filled with a pale steady light that buzzed from the overhead fluorescents. A veil of rain shimmered down the high windows, and crushed ice rattled from the mouths of vending machines. It was me and Allison Downey and Mollie Wicks and John Peacock and Lelah Holeman and Robert Shriver.

"Most likely to the hospital," I said. "They wheeled him down the hall on a gurney, and that's the last we saw of him."

Robert Shriver pinched his sandwich bag shut along the zipper. "I was watching when he fell," he said. "It was mostly shock, I think. The bucket just barely tapped him, and the glass didn't cut him at all. To tell you the truth, I almost laughed when it happened: I mean, a bucket—who would figure?" He swept a few crumbs to the floor. "He'll probably be back on Monday."

I had seen the faces of the paramedics as they left our room—they had looked like soap bubbles draining of color—and I knew that he wouldn't be back any time soon.

"Let's talk about something else," I said, swallowing the last of my sandwich.

In the weeks since my mother had left home, my father had grown concerned about my diet. Each morning before he went to work, he wrapped my lunch in a brown paper bag and left it for me on the kitchen counter—a peanut butter and sprout sandwich, a bag of coarse blue corn chips, a red apple drizzled with green, and a sealed tray of crackers with pocked yellow cheese and a spread wand.

I never ate the apple.

Every day I swaddled it in my napkin and backpack with the thought that I might eat it on the bus, and every day I threw it in the garbage when I got home. I planted it beneath chicken bones and paper towels, depleted tins of cat food and packets of soured condiments, in the hope that my father would not find it.

Mollie Wicks was attempting to untwine the decorative white icing atop her chocolate cupcake. "When my grandma died," she said, "we held the services in our living room. I wanted to see her, but my mom wouldn't let me—she sent me to stay with the neighbors." She paused, ticking at her fingernail, and her gaze seemed to split its focus. "I was only three or four at the time, and I'd never known anyone else who died. I tangled her up with God somehow. I used to imagine God sitting in Heaven with frizzled gray hair and my grandmother's blue flower nightgown."

John Peacock, spooning up dollops of pudding, told us a story about his uncle, who cared for him when his parents were fighting. His uncle, he said, kept the grounds at the Rivergarden cemetery. A few years ago he had found one of the burial vaults split open. Sod and concrete were everywhere, and the tombstone was rent in two. He reported it as an act of vandalism. Then, a week later, it happened again. He was weeding the fenceline when he heard a sound like the sudden *whoompf* of a gas fire. Fragments of soil rained down around him. An ash sapling landed at his shoulder. The yard was otherwise deserted. "It turns out," said John, "that some of the caskets were sealed too tight. Bacteria was filling them with pressure. They blew open like bombs."

"Weird," said Lelah. Behind her, a vending machine stopped with a quick little shudder.

"My mom," said Allison, "told me once that she thinks my grandma was reborn as a cat. She died when Mom was in college, before I was born, and that's supposed to be one of the last things she said—that she would come back as a cat. The story goes that exactly one year after my grandmother died, my mom opened the door to find a cat on the stoop. She carried the cat inside, and fed it, and ended up keeping it as a pet." Allison plucked at the ribs of a plastic fork. "The strange thing about all this is that Mom's parents never really liked cats. My grandmother was apparently a dog person."

"What happened to her?" asked John Peacock.

"The cat? She was killed by a car, I think. That's not part of the story, though." Allison blew a twist of hair from her eye. "She also knocked down the birdcage once and ate my mom's canary," she said. "Uncle William."

A tiny wry smile flickered over her lips.

Outside, a sudden gust of hail came rattling across the windows.

"What about you, Jeremy?" Allison shifted under the table, and the tail of her skirt swept into my leg. "Have you known anyone who's died?"

I could hear Walter Bozeman at another table delivering a pun he had heard—the effectual phrase was "kicking the bucket"—and I could hear his squirrelly friends laughing and nibbling potato chips.

"No," I said. My leg was tingling with suppressed motion; I was afraid that if I moved, Allison would notice me and withdraw her skirt. "No, this is my first."

Allison tucked her hair behind her ear and bit into a chunk of pineapple, a thread of which remained on the curve of her lower lip. John Peacock pressed his finger to the top of a drinking straw, suspending a column of bubbling root beer inside. Lelah Holeman buttered a muffin and Robert Shriver licked a tootsie-pop and Mollie Wicks took a salami with her sharp white teeth.

The front panel of a coke machine was shining with a silver haze inside my apple. I cupped it in my palm and displayed it to the table. "Does anyone want this?" I asked.

The bell rang and they all shook their heads.

Let me tell you about Allison Downey.

In the Monday morning assembly at which we began our seventh-grade year, I sat behind a girl I hadn't seen before. She was wearing a lake-red pullover with a dangling hood, and her collar dipped at the root of her neck, revealing a little chain of vertebrae. During the morning prayer I followed this ridge of bone with my eyes, sliding occasionally into her hood, then climbing to her collar like some tiny mountaineer. We stood and sat for the pledge of allegiance, and Principal Raymer took the microphone for his introductory address. When I noticed a loose hair on the girl's shoulder, a certain tidiness in me insisted that I remove it. I remember feeling anxious and slightly abashed as I reached out my hand. The instant I touched her she turned around. I started in my chair and, coloring, presented the hair to her. I expected to be met with a show of irritation, but I wasn't. Instead, she signaled me near, then demonstrated something to me that I have not since forgotten: how if you hold a hair taut and draw your fingers toward the root, it will make a short, thin sound like the hum of a spinning top.

This was Allison.

Allison wore long sheer skirts that rustled against her shoes, and she spoke in a scramble of words when she was nervous. She walked down the stairways of our school like a demonstration of motion, her left hand sweeping the banister and her feet skipping the final step. (She took great pleasure, I think, in practiced gestures like these—blindly shutting a familiar door, perfectly striking a matchbook match.) I had three classes with her that year: earth science, English, and geography. One evening, as we sat in her bedroom plotting a posterboard map of Brazil (an assignment for Mister Ullom's geography class), a small down feather floated from my winter coat and settled on the fringe of her eyelashes; we worked for half an hour before she noticed it. One afternoon as she waited for the bus, she found a woolly orange caterpillar bunching and elongating over her sandal, and when she showed it to John Peacock, he stepped on it. She glowered silently at him for the next three days. At the last football game of our seventh-grade year, a night when the cold shaped our words into little white mushroom puffs, I asked her if she wanted a drink from the concessions stand, and after a prolonged quiet, she said that she'd been thinking recently about the difference between *good guilt* and *bad guilt* and that though she wasn't sure, and there was certainly room for disagreement, she thought that she might have a lot of bad guilt. I hid a smile and arched my eyebrows at Matt Newton. Allison began to say something, muffled herself, and nodded. "You know what I'm sick of?" she said after a moment. "I'm sick of significant glances." And when she seethed off through the bleachers, I hurried behind her to apologize.

Allison collected glass snowstorm balls, which she kept in neat rows on the shelves of her bedroom. I remember shaking them with her and watching the water churn inside: what would it be like, we wondered, to live in such a place—a home that might stagger and right itself, a silver eruption of snow? She liked to walk through the revolving doors of shopping malls and multistory office buildings without touching the partitions, and she could do this with such casual grace that it seemed as if she were simply passing through an empty doorway, sheets of glass whirling around her. Once on Halloween she gave me a plastic ring crowned with a flared orange spider, and I wore it like a talisman until its band split in the laundry.

Allison lived with her mother and small brother (her father was remarried). She was careful and muddled and dreaming and lovely. And though she would move with her family one winter to the forests and slate-blue skies of the Pacific Northwest, and I would not see her again, for a long time I believed in my sleep that I was still living in those months and years, awakening with the thought that she'd be waiting in the lunchroom.

That afternoon, while we were waiting to hear about Coach Schramm, the wind carried the rain away over the mud-brown river. The air took on a glassiness that made each object seem sharp-edged and bright, wholly contained within itself. From my algebra and health classes, I watched trees and concrete parking stones glistening with daylight.

An aluminum can rolled back and forth on the sidewalk, and a blackened tree limb lay in the grass. Cars and the reflections of cars passed down the highway in a jet of standing water.

We were scheduled to have a pep rally at the end of the day, but whispers suggested that Coach Schramm had not pulled through, and the prospect of organized chants and the clapping of hands led Principal Raymer to cancel the event. Instead, when the bell rang for seventh period, we found ourselves congregating outside the gymnasium and cafeteria, waiting in the lobby for our parents or freely wandering the hallways: this was something that never happened in our school, but on that day it did. Allison and I decided to head for the bluff overlooking the highway. As we walked around the building she ran her hand along the brick wall, tracing the rise and fall of a line of mortar. "It's like bobbing over the ocean," she said, and I wasn't sure whether she was referring to the motion of her fingers along the brickwork or to some other, more interior current.

The office secretary, Miss Vickery, was emptying a three-hole puncher into the trash can: she held it like a ketchup bottle, jiggling it back and forth, and punched holes drifted from her hands like snow. She said nothing to us. Mister Toothman, the school custodian, was collecting fragments of glass from beneath the window cleaner's scaffold; a damp washrag trailed from the pocket of his slacks, flashing up and down in the breeze.

We settled in together against the shank of a mossy stone.

Allison began tearing at the flesh of a leaf, exposing the thin yellow delta of its veins. "What makes you think of me?" she asked, touching my side with her elbow.

I thought for a moment and said, "I'm not sure." In truth, I didn't understand the question, and I could see that she heard this in my voice.

"I think of you, for instance, when the phone rings on the hour, because you always call on the hour," she said. "And I think of you when I ride on escalators, because you told me they scared you when you were a kid. I think of you when I go to that restaurant where I saw you with your parents or when I hear that ridiculous fish-heads song you always sing. When I look at my snowstorm globes, I think of you shining the flashlight through them, and the pattern of the snow against the wall."

She hiccuped and pressed a hand to her chest.

"I think of you when I see ducks," she said. "Or sign language. Or shadow puppets."

"Why's that?"

"You do this thing with your hand sometimes." She bent and swiveled her own hand like the head of a periscope. "You talk with it," she said, flapping her fingers against the ball of her thumb.

This was true, but I decided to deny it. "No, I don't."

"Yes," said Allison, "you do."

"No." I shook my head. "You must be confusing me with someone else."

"You don't recognize *this*?" The duckbill of Allison's hand met my eyes with a steely gaze. *"Hello,"* it said. *"My name's Jeremy."* When I laughed, it dispersed into its constituent fingers.

"So," said Allison, "what makes you think of me?"

I could hear the first of the afternoon buses rumbling into the parking lot on the far side of the building, and taking a small breath, I said something that caught me off guard: "I think of you when I fail." The look that came into Allison's eyes was sad and certain and unsurprised, and it gave me a plunging feeling inside.

"No," I said. I wanted to explain. "Sometimes I panic. I'll blow a test, or ruin something important, or say something wrong, and suddenly I'll think that it's too late—it's all over. I'll really believe this. And then I think of you and it slows me down: I think, if Allison's here, there's probably still time."

A smile evanesced across her face, and we fell into a silence.

From the field below us came a flicker of blue. A man in nightclothes emerged from a spinney of trees, looked around furtively, and stole away toward the interstate. I watched him linger by a pool of rainwater, its surface bristling with onion grass. Then he vanished behind an adjacent slope. Our school was separated from a hospital for troubled youth by a mile of woodland and brambles. Often, escaped patients would appear on our parking lot, their pants and slippers black with mud, and through the window we would see them taking cover in the bushes or roaming between the faculty cars. They wore dreamy expressions and light blue pajamas, as if some fragment of the sky had suddenly found itself alive, and human, and in our parking lot.

Sitting on the hillside, I watched the man in his nightclothes reappear, cross the gravel skirting of the highway, and thumb a ride from a passing truck.

Allison was fashioning a hummock of leaves on my right thigh. She shaped it carefully with the cushions of her palms, piercing it with an occasional green twig to brace it up and pin it together. I could feel her fingers darting and skimming over my leg. "There," she said, crowning the stack with a snug little pine cone. She flicked the dirt from her hands as if testing the temperature of a stove.

"Above," she said. This was one of the words we had been asked to practice for our preposition exam. "The pine cone," she said, "is above the leaves."

"Are you ready for that?" I asked.

"I think so," said Allison. "I'll study some more tonight."

The sun slipped briefly behind a cloud, and a blackbird shot past us with a sudden *vabap* of its wings.

I aimed my finger at the leaf arrangement. "Beneath," I said. "The leaves are beneath the pine cone."

Allison nodded.

"On," she said. "The leaves and the pine cone are on your leg."

"Off," I said. I took the stack in my hands—it was the size and weight of a cupcake—and gingerly set it aside. "Not any more."

Allison tugged at her skirt. "Through," she said. She leaned to one side. "The ground is soaking through my clothes."

I had been planning to offer the same preposition, and before I could think of another, she interrupted me: "Before," she grinned. "I got to the next one before you."

"And I got there *after* you."

"Next to," she said, and she edged closer to me, slipping over the bell nuts and the fallen leaves until her leg touched my own. My throat went dry and I swallowed. "Allison is next to Jeremy," she said.

I raised my hand, signaling her to pay attention, then demonstrated my next preposition by watching her in pantomime—I began at her shoes and her ankles, and laddered from there to her knees and waist and neck. "Well?" I asked.

A sheltering oak began to rustle in the breeze. She shook her head. "I have no idea."

"Regarding," I said.

"Aaah—" Her voice gave a trill. "Pretty clever." She folded her arms around me, clasping her hands at my shoulder.

"And this," she said, "is around."

A little *hm* of surprise escaped my throat. "About," I said—and holding tight, I repeated her gesture.

"Toward," she said.

"Beside," I said.

"Across."

"Near."

"Against."

The far side of the school hummed with the voices of parents and idling cars. My temple was pressed to Allison's, my arm to her back, the turn of my face to the turn of her own. She shifted her weight, and her jacket rucked together at my side. She brought her teeth together, and I felt the motion of them against the pad of her cheek. When she blinked and drew toward me, parting her lips, my heart tumbled over inside me like an hourglass.

"Betwixt," she said.

Though some prefer the spring, with its split cocoons and dandelion meadows; or the lazy, boundless days of summer, with a sun that drifts past like a great open eye; or the winter, harsh and deep and pure, with its living room trees and its husk of white snow—though some prefer the newer months, I've always been drawn to the fall. In the fall, we step outside and everything comes toward us. Early morning lawns are silver with frost, and breezes sweep past tree trunks with a robust whistle. Flocks of birds segment and join in the sky. Grassant snakes slither on their bellies through the leaves. People wear jackets and huddle together. The summer belongs to the sky, I think, and the winter belongs to the ground. The spring belongs to nature and the physical world. The fall, though—it belongs to us: the fall belongs to women and men.

That afternoon, as the school bus hurried me past the bluff and the river, I bent my head to the window and let the glass shiver against my forehead. The sunlight was slanting through the clouds in visible bands, and a manhole cover shone from the sidewalk like a new coin. Leaves went eddying into the air from beneath our tires. I was thinking of Allison. A line of sparrows perched on a telephone wire and I envisioned them rising and settling in position, bird by bird like a row of dominoes, as my voice buzzed past them that evening on the hour.

Martha Newton jabbed me with her elbow. "What are you beaming about?" she asked.

We eased to a stop at a traffic light. I answered, "Basic grammar."

Across the aisle, Kelly Schramm, Coach Schramm's eldest daughter, was pressing her hand to the window. Behind her the Goosen brothers, Mark and Simon, were laughing mutedly at some secret joke. Every time their voices barked, Kelly started. She searched the sky with small worried glances.

I buttoned my jacket as we approached the bus stop and hoisted my backpack onto my shoulder. I walked home kicking a small gray chunk of asphalt. House keys in hand, I stepped through the front door.

On my way to the bedroom, I stopped in the kitchen. The white linoleum floor was glistening with water, laces and streaks of it drying in the yellow sun. A mop and bucket stood alongside the refrigerator, and a torn-open trash bag lay on the counter. Beside the trash bag, between the bread box and the toaster, sat six dented apples. They were as red and luminous and distinct as signal buoys.

I heard the voice of my father walking down the hallway.

"Is that you, Jeremy?" he called. "We need to have a talk."

A Day in the Life of Half of Rumpelstiltskin

7:45 a.m. He showers and dresses.

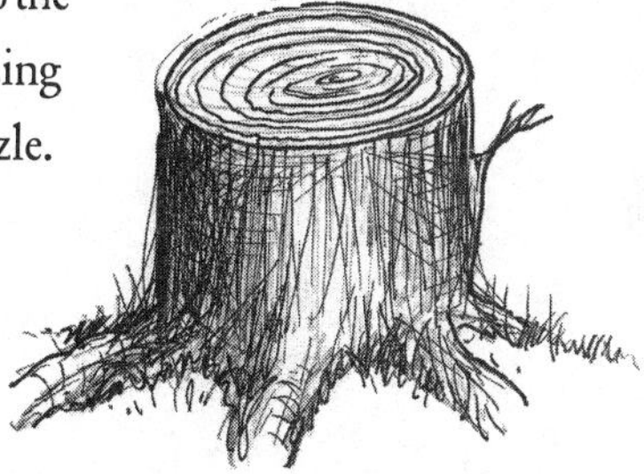

Half of Rumpelstiltskin awakens from a dream in which his body is a filament of straw, coiled and twined about itself so as to mimic the presence of flesh and entrails, of hands and ribs and muscles and a knotty, throbbing heart. In his dream, Half of Rumpelstiltskin is seated at a spinning wheel, his foot pumping furiously at the treadle, his body winding into gold around the spindle. He unravels top down—from the crown of his head to the unclipped edge of his big toenail—loosing a fog of dust and a moist, vegetal drizzle. When the last of him whisks from the treadle and into the air, he is gold, through and through. He lies there perfect, glinting, and altogether gone. Half of Rumpelstiltskin is the whole of the picture and nowhere in it. He is beautiful, and remunerative, and he isn't even there to see it. Half of Rumpelstiltskin has spun himself empty. There is nothing of him left.

When Half of Rumpelstiltskin awakens, there is nothing of him right. He is like a pentagram folded across its center or a tree split by lightning. He is like the left half of a slumberous manikin, yawning and shuddering, rising from within the netlike architecture of his dreams. He is like that *exactly.* Half of Rumpelstiltskin sleeps in a child's trundle bed. He turns down his linens and his thick, abrasive woolen blanket and hops to the bathroom.

Half of Rumpelstiltskin moves from point to point—bed to bathroom, *a* to *b*—in one of two ways. Either he hops on one foot, his left, or he arches his body to walk from toe to palm and palm to toe. When he hops, Half of Rumpelstiltskin lands on the flat of his foot, leaning backward to counter his momentum, which for many years pitched him straight to the floor. When he walks, Half of Rumpelstiltskin looks as might a banana with feet at both ends. Through the years, he has learned to plod and pace and shuffle, to shamble and saunter and stride. Half of Rumpelstiltskin doesn't own a car, and there's never been anyone to carry him.

In the shower, Half of Rumpelstiltskin scours himself with a bar of marbled green soap, a washcloth, and—for the skin at his extremities, as stubborn and scabrous as bark—a horsehair scrub brush. He lathers. He rinses. He dries himself with a plush cotton towel, sousing the water from his pancreas and his ligaments and the spongy marrow in the cavity of his sternum. Half of Rumpelstiltskin is the only man he knows whose forearm is a hard-to-reach place.

Outside his window, the sky is a startled blue, from horizon to horizon interrupted only by a dissipating jet trail and a bespotment of soaring birds. The jet trail is of uniform thickness all along its length, and try as he might, Half of Rumpelstiltskin can spot a jet at neither end. He runs his forefinger along the window sash, then flattens his palm against the pane. Both are warm and dry. Although it's only the beginning of March, Half of Rumpelstiltskin decides to dress lightly—skullcap and a tawny brown slacks leg, a button-up shirt and a red canvas sneaker.

Before leaving for work, Half of Rumpelstiltskin brews a pot of coffee. He drinks it with a lump of sugar and a dash of half-and-half. The coffee bores through him like a colony of chittering termites—gnawing down the trunk of him, devouring the wood of his dreams. As he drinks, Half of Rumpelstiltskin watches a children's variety show on public television. The monster puppets are his favorite, with their blue fur, their ravenous appetites, and their whirling eyes. The children laugh at the monsters' jokes and ask them about the alphabet, and the monsters hug the children with their two pendent arms.

9:05 a.m. He goes to work.

Half of Rumpelstiltskin works three hours every morning, until noon, standing in for missing or vandalized mannequins at a department store in a nearby strip mall. Until recently he worked in the warehouse, processing orders, cataloging merchandise, and inspecting enormous cardboard boxes with rusted staples the size of his pinkie finger. Lately, however, a spate of mannequin thefts—the result, police suspect, of a gang initiation ritual—has left local shopping centers dispossessed of display models, and Half of Rumpelstiltskin has been transferred in to fill the void. He considers this ironic.

—You're five minutes late, his boss tells him when he arrives. Don't let it happen again.

Half of Rumpelstiltskin's boss smells of cigar smoke and seafood.

—And from now on, I expect to see you clean-shaven when you come in, he says gruffly. Nobody likes a hairy mannequin. Now get changed and get to work.

Half of Rumpelstiltskin nods in reply. Cod, he thinks.

Half of Rumpelstiltskin soon emerges from the wardrobe wearing a junior-size vinyl jumpsuit with a zippered front and a designer label. Around his head is swathed a stocking cap several sizes too large for him. It rests heavy on his eyebrow and plunges to the small of his back in broad, rambling folds. His jumpsuit, on its right side, is as flaccid as the inner tube of a flat tire. Half of Rumpelstiltskin takes his place between two cold, trendy mannequins—one slate gray with both arms halved at the elbow, its head severed as if by a huntsman's ax from right ear to left jawbone, and the other a metal figure composed of flat geometric shapes with a polished black sheen, jointed together with transparent rods to resemble the human form. Half of Rumpelstiltskin feels himself a true and vital part of the society of mannequins. With them, he fits right in.

An adolescent with close-cropped hair, a pierced eyebrow, and a scar extending like a smile from the corner of his lip to the prominence of his cheek approaches Half of Rumpelstiltskin near the end of his shift. Half of Rumpelstiltskin stands as still as a tree in the hope that the boy will walk past, but instead he circles and draws closer, like a dog bound to him by a chain. Upon reaching the platform where Half of Rumpelstiltskin stands, the boy threads his arm through the jumpsuit's empty leg and takes hold of Half of Rumpelstiltskin's spleen. He appears surprised. He removes his hand—spleenless—and sniffs it. Shrugging, he reaches again for the jumpsuit's empty cuff.

I wouldn't do that if I were you, says Half of Rumpelstiltskin, and the boy backs calmly away. He stops, crooks his neck, and looks quizzically into Half of Rumpelstiltskin's eye. Then he brushes his fingers along the underside of his jaw and flicks them past the nub of his chin. His eyes glare scornfully at Half of Rumpelstiltskin. He strides confidently away, as if nothing at all has happened. Half of Rumpelstiltskin watches him exit the building through a pair of sliding glass doors. His boss steps out from behind a carousel hung with heavy flannel shirts.

—What was that all about? he asks.

Nothing, responds Half of Rumpelstiltskin.

—No fraternization with the customers. You should know better than that.

Okay, says Half of Rumpelstiltskin.

His boss shakes his head disapprovingly and, turning to leave, mutters under his breath.

—Fool, he whispers. Meathead. Hayseed. Half-wit.

Half of Rumpelstiltskin checks his wristwatch. It's quitting time.

12:15 p.m. He eats lunch in the park.

Beside the wooden bench on which he sits is a tree stump, its hollow banked with wood pulp and a few faded soda cans. Half of Rumpelstiltskin can't help but wonder what has become of the tree itself. A year ago it rose within the park, housing the sky, a thousand tatters of blue, within its overspread branches. Now it is gone, and this bench is here in its place. Possibly the bench itself was once a part of the tree—hewn, perhaps, from its thickset trunk—but if so, what has become of the rest? The only certainty is that it fell, releasing from its branches a host of harried birds and vagrant squirrels, galaxies and planets and the sure and vaulting sky. With so much restless weight between its leaves, it could just as well have burst like a balloon. *When you're trying to hold the sky inside you,* thinks Half of Rumpelstiltskin, *something is bound to fail. The sky is inevitable. The sky is a foregone conclusion.* Overhead, the sun pulses behind swells of heat, wobbling like an egg yolk. The jet trail has dispersed, blown ragged by the winds of early March.

Half of Rumpelstiltskin watches as, in the distance, a kite mounts its way into the air. Beneath it, a man stands in a meadow of dry yellow grass, unspooling a length of string. He tugs at the kite and the kite tugs back, yanking the man in fits and starts through the field and toward a playground. Half of Rumpelstiltskin sees children loosed from the plate of a restless, wheeling merry-go-round, holding to its metal bars with both arms, their bodies like streamers in the air. He sees swings arcing up and down and supine parents reading newspapers and smoking cigarettes. Beside the playground, a sandwich stand sprouts from the ground like a toadstool. Half of Rumpelstiltskin's stomach churns at the sight of it, rumbling like sneakers caught in a spin cycle. He places his hand against its interior lining, finds it dry and clean and webbed like ceiling insulation. Half of Rumpelstiltskin is hungry.

At the sandwich stand, he asks for peanut butter and jelly on wheat. Eating and hopping, he unwittingly lights on an anthill. It goes scattering ahead of him in a fine particulate brume. Half of Rumpelstiltskin lowers himself to the ground and sits with his haunch on his heel. He watches as ants swarm from the razed hill: they broadcast themselves in all directions, like bursting fireworks or ink on water. Within a matter of minutes, the tiny, volatile creatures have built a protective ring of dirt around the bore above their home. Half of Rumpelstiltskin finds the sight of creatures working as a collective a strange and unfamiliar one. It's spooky and—for some reason—a little bit sad. Half of Rumpelstiltskin has trouble enough comprehending the nature of individuality without throwing intersubjectivity into the pot. Although he has unmade anthills on many, many occasions, Half of Rumpelstiltskin has never stayed to watch the ants rebuild. As a gesture of good will, he leaves them that portion of his sandwich he has not yet swallowed. If they can't eat it, he thinks, perhaps they can build with it.

An abundance of drugstores line the walk between the park and Half of Rumpelstiltskin's home, and he stops at one along the way. There he purchases a chocolate bar, a bottle of apple-green mouthwash, and a newspaper from the metroplex across the river, the headlines of which affirm what he has long held to be true—that the world tumbles its way through political conventions, economic treaties, televised sporting events, and invasive military tactics in starving third-world nations with utter indifference to the inglorious fact of his half-existence. The stock market columns report that gold is down—straw way, way down.

Half of Rumpelstiltskin has poor depth perception. Hopping home, he trips over a concrete parking block.

1:25 p.m. He receives a Mad-Libs letter from his other Half.

3 March ________
(year)

Half of Rumpelstiltskin:

Not much new here in ____________________. The ______________
(place where you are not) (term of derision)

Queen has decided once again to levy a whole new batch of taxes—and guess who the ________________ (ironic adjective) victims are this time around: homunculi. That's right. Miss ______________ (what's her name) has decided that the time is ripe to tax _______ (things), _______ (other things), _______, and homunculi. And who's the *only* homunculus on this whole __________ (color) ____________ (landmass)?

Me! Rumpel-____________________ (crude participial adjective)-stiltskin . . . Sorry. Just need to vent some of my ______________ (bodily organ) and frustration. I should learn to control my temper—if there's a moral to this whole affair, that must be it—but you know how it gets. ____________ (Tame interjection), at least we're not as bad as ____ (fictional character renowned for losing his or her temper to no good end).

Life on the personal front is no ____________________ (word that rhymes with *letter*) than on the political. I'm still out of work— the ______________ (occupation) position fell through—and I'm on the outs with ____ (person you and I know who used to keep me from being lonely sometimes). Sometimes I wonder when and how it all turned so ______________________________ (adjective expressing disconsolation).

When you get the chance, ________________ (direction) your half of this

____________________ to me, so I can find out what I've written.
(word that rhymes with *better*)

When the words won't come to me, I figure they must be yours. I miss you and ____________ ____________ ____________.
(subject) (verb) (object)

____________. ________________.
(sad word) (sad, sad, sad, sad word)

All Right:
Half of Rumpelstiltskin

2:30 p.m. He delivers a speech to a local women's auxiliary organization.

Half of Rumpelstiltskin stands at a lectern fashioned of fluted, burnished cherry wood and speaks on "The Birthrights of First-Born Children," a topic in which he claims no small degree of expertise. Half of Rumpelstiltskin has had his fair share of ill-favored dealings with first-born children, particularly those of millers' daughters. As he speaks, the cheery, preoccupied faces before him exchange knowing glances and subtle pointed smiles. Half of Rumpelstiltskin, when asked to address this meeting, was not informed as to whether the auxiliary was *for* or *against* first-born children and their concomitant birthrights—and so he has taken what he considers to be a nonpartisan slant on the topic. Listening to the raspy coughs of the women in the audience and regarding their nodding, oblate heads, he can't decide whether he is offending or boring them. Half of Rumpelstiltskin concludes his speech to a smattering of polite applause that sounds like the last few popping kernels in a bag of prebuttered popcorn. When he steps out from behind the lectern and joins the women in the audience for a question-

and-answer session, nobody has a thing to say about first-born children, birthrights, red pottage, or the nation of Israel. Instead, as he might have suspected, it's all *straw-to-gold* this and *fairy tale* that.

—What, the women ask, happened to your other half?

I split myself in two, says Half of Rumpelstiltskin, *when the Queen guessed my name. However,* he says, *that's a story that demands a discussion of first-born children. So then—*

—But, the women ask, *how* did you split yourself in two?

In a fit of anger, says Half of Rumpelstiltskin. *When the Queen guessed my name, I stamped explosively, burying my right leg to the waist beneath the floorboards. In trying to unearth myself, I took hold of my left foot, wrenching it so hard that I split down the center. My other half lives overseas. I myself emigrated.*

—I thought, say the women, that upon stamping the ground you fell to the center of the earth. Or that you merely bruised your heel and wandered off in a fit of malaise.

No, says Half of Rumpelstiltskin, *those are just myths.*

—Is it true, ask the women, that you wish to huff and puff and blow our houses down?

No, says Half of Rumpelstiltskin. *You're thinking of the Big Bad Wolf.*

—Is it true what we hear about you and the girl with the grandmother?

No. That, too, is the Big Bad Wolf.

—Is it true that you'd like to cook our children in your large, cast-iron stewpot?

Half of Rumpelstiltskin sighs. *No,* he says, *I am in fact a strict vegetarian.*

—Do you believe in the interdependence of name and identity? ask the women.

Yes, I do.

—Why don't you change your name?

Because I'm still Rumpelstiltskin, says Half of Rumpelstiltskin. *I'm just not* all *of him.*

—You're still Rumpelstiltskin? Even after having lived as Half, and only half, of Rumpelstiltskin for oh-so-many years?

Yes.

—Is there a moral to all of this?

No. Half of Rumpelstiltskin checks his watch. *No, there isn't. I have time for one more question.*

—If you were granted only one wish, ask the women, what would you wish for?

Half of Rumpelstiltskin doesn't miss a beat. *Bilateral symmetry,* he says.

4:10 p.m. He shops for dinner at the grocery store.

Half of Rumpelstiltskin is standing in line at the checkout counter of a supermarket, reading the cover of a tabloid newspaper upon which is pictured a pair of Siamese twins and an infant the size of a walnut—who is actually curled, in the photograph, next to a walnut. The infant looks like the protean, half-formed bird Half of Rumpelstiltskin once saw when he split open a nested egg, and through his gelate, translucent skin is visible the kernel of a heart. The caption above the child claims that he was born without a brain. Half of Rumpelstiltskin, inching forward in line, finds himself thinking about the responsibilities delegated to either hemisphere of the brain. If, as they say, the right half of the brain controls the left half of the body—and the left half the right—Half of Rumpelstiltskin moves and talks, yawns and dances, under the edicts of the other Half of

Rumpelstiltskin's portion of Rumpelstiltskin's brain. Is it possible, Half of Rumpelstiltskin wonders, that he is somewhere across the ocean, sitting in front of a fireplace or reading a magazine, operating under the delusion that he is standing here in the supermarket, buying ingredients for his evening's meal and looking at the tabloids? That through half a world's measure of Rumpelstiltskin-lessness, he sends directives, receives impressions, down a sequence of nodes and fibers concealed within the dense, gordian anatomy of the earth—and his other half the same? That he is never where he thinks he is or heading where he hopes to be?

Half of Rumpelstiltskin sometimes feels absolutely and undeniably alienated from everyone and everything around him.

Asleep in the shopping cart in front of him, her head resting upon the pocked rind of a firm green cantaloupe, a baby lies beside a bag of crinkle-cut potato wedges. She is breathing softly through her nose, and her dark, wavy hair frames the pudge of her face. As the Halves of Rumpelstiltskin told the Queen when she offered the treasures of the kingdom in exchange for her first-born child, something living is more important to him than all the treasures in the world. The baby gurgles, her legs poking through the bars of the shopping cart, and pulls to her stomach a round of Gouda cheese the size of her hand. He would never have imagined, not for a heartbeat, that children were so easily come by. Had he known you could buy them at the supermarket, his life might not have become the mess it is today.

He watches as the woman in front of him purchases her groceries—potatoes and cheese, leafy vegetables and globose, pulpous fruits, several green plastic bottles of soda, a wedge of ham garnished with pineapple, and the baby—and wheels them to the parking lot. As the woman at the register of the checkout lane scans his groceries above a brilliant red scattering of light, Half of Rumpelstiltskin leafs through his wallet looking for a form of photo identification and a major credit card. On his license he is pictured before a screen of powder blue. His head is tilted by a slim margin to the left, and looking closely he can just begin to see the white edge of his upper incisor and a sliver of cortical sponge. Half of Rumpelstiltskin was pleased to find that he was not grinning in his license photo. People who grin, he has always thought, look squirrelly and eccentric, sometimes barking mad, and, on occasion, dangerous and inconsonant—as if they're trying to hide something from the world, something virulent and bitter on the surface of their tongues. People whose teeth show in license photos are most often just the eccentric sort—but never completely harmless. Half of Rumpelstiltskin had half a mind to return his own when he found that he could spot the edge of his upper incisor.

Half of Rumpelstiltskin pays the checkout attendant. He grasps his grocery sacks by their cutting plastic grips, hefts them over his shoulder, and hops through a set of yawning, automatic doors.

5:50 p.m. He cooks supper and dances a jig.

In his kitchen sits an outsize black cauldron, like a bubble blown by the mouth of the scullery floor. It is a few heads taller than Half of Rumpelstiltskin himself, and to see over its lip he must climb to the top tread of a stepladder propped against its side. From the brim of the cauldron spumes a thick, pallid yeast, and across its pitchy interior are layers of burnt and crusted food. Half of Rumpelstiltskin stands at the cutting board with a finely edged knife, dicing onions, potatoes, and peppers into small, palmate segments. He scrapes these into a tin basin, adds spices and a queer lumpish mass that he pulls from his freezer, and hops up the stepladder to dump them into the cauldron. The vegetables, pitched into the stew, churn beneath its surface, interrupting the reddish brown paste that thickens there into a skin.

Half of Rumpelstiltskin hops down to the kitchen floor. He washes his hand in the sink, then dries it on his slacks. Half of Rumpelstiltskin is pleased by the prospect of supper. He considers himself a true gourmand.

As is his custom prior to eating, Half of Rumpelstiltskin crooks himself from toe to palm and reels around his cauldron. Sometimes he holds his ankle in his hand and hoops his way through the kitchen; sometimes he cambers at the waist, bucking from head to toe like a seesaw. Half of Rumpelstiltskin dances, and hungers, and sings his dancing and hungering song—his voice ululating like that of a hound crying for its master:

Dancing dances, brewing feasts,
Won't restore me in the least.
Brewing feasts and singing songs,
Nights are slow and days are long.
Lamentation! Drudgery!
Half of Rumpelstiltskin's me.

10:35 p.m. He falls asleep watching *The Dating Game*.

Half of Rumpelstiltskin grows listless after heavy meals. In the bathroom, he rasps his mossy teeth with a fibrillar plastic brush until they feel smooth against his tongue. He gargles with his apple-green mouthwash, tilting his head there-side down so as not to dribble into the cavity of his body. Half of Rumpelstiltskin urinates, watching as a pale yellow fluid courses the length of his urethra into the toilet. Afterward he leaves the seat up.

On his way to the couch, Half of Rumpelstiltskin presses his palm against the pane of a window. It's growing chilly outside. He retrieves an eiderdown quilt from the linen closet and settles in beneath it.

A man with brown hair—hair that rises above his forehead like a wave collapsing toward his crown—grins on the television. He speaks in sunny, urgent tones to a woman who looks to be about a half-bubble off-level. The woman is charged with the task of choosing a date from among three dapper men who introduce themselves as if there's something inside them gone empty without her. She asks the men a question, and they answer to a swell of applause from the studio audience. Name one word that describes the sky, says the woman. It's high, says one man. It's wide, says another. It's inevitable, says the third. Half of Rumpelstiltskin is rooting for the third.

The people on the television seem lost. Somewhere, at some point, they forgot who they were or how to be happy. They found themselves wandering around behind the haze of their fear and desire. They stumbled into his television. The lucky ones will walk off with one another, out of his television set and onto some beach beneath a soft and falling sun, heady with the confidence that they've found someone—another voice, a pair of arms—to be happy with. Half of Rumpelstiltskin wishes them the best, but he knows something they don't—which perhaps they never will—something that may not even be true for them. He knows that it happens in this world that you can change in such a way as to never again be complete, that you can lose parts of who you once were—and sometimes you'll get better, but sometimes you'll never be anything more than fractional: than who you once were, a few parts hollow. He knows that sometimes what's missing isn't somebody else.

Half of Rumpelstiltskin sinks into sleep like a leaf subsiding to the floor of the moon. When next he opens his eye, the television will whisper behind a face of lambent snow.

The Ceiling

There was a sky that day, sun-rich and open and blue. A raft of silver clouds was floating along the horizon, and robins and sparrows were calling from the trees. It was my son Joshua's seventh birthday and we were celebrating in our back yard. He and the children were playing on the swing set, and Melissa and I were sitting on the deck with the parents. Earlier that afternoon, a balloon and gondola had risen from the field at the end of our block, sailing past us with an exhalation of fire. Joshua told his friends that he knew the pilot. "His name is Mister Clifton," he said, as they tilted their heads back and slowly revolved in place. "I met him at the park last year. He took me into the air with him and let me drop a soccer ball into a swimming pool. We almost hit a helicopter. He told me he'd come by on my birthday." Joshua shielded his eyes against the sun. "Did you see him wave?" he asked. "He just waved at me."

This was a story.

The balloon drifted lazily away, turning to expose each delta and crease of its fabric, and we listened to the children resuming their play. Mitch Nauman slipped his sunglasses into his shirt pocket. "Ever notice how kids their age will handle a toy?" he said. Mitch was our next-door neighbor. He was the single father of Bobby Nauman, Joshua's strange best friend. His other best friend, Chris Boschetti, came from a family of cosmetics executives. My wife had taken to calling them "Rich and Strange."

Mitch pinched the front of his shirt between his fingers and fanned himself with it. "The actual function of the toy is like some sort of obstacle," he said. "They'll dream up a new use for everything in the world."

I looked across the yard at the swing set: Joshua was trying to shinny up one of the A-poles; Taylor Tugwell and Sam Yoo were standing on the teeter swing; Adam Smithee was tossing fistfuls of pebbles onto the slide and watching them rattle to the ground.

My wife tipped one of her sandals onto the grass with the ball of her foot. "Playing as you should isn't Fun," she said: "it's Design."

She parted her toes around the front leg of Mitch's lawn chair. He leaned back into the sunlight, and her calf muscles tautened.

My son was something of a disciple of flying things. On his bedroom wall were posters of fighter planes and wild birds. A model of a helicopter was chandeliered to his ceiling. His birthday cake, which sat before me on the picnic table, was decorated with a picture of a rocket ship—a silver white missile with discharging thrusters. I had been hoping that the baker would place a few stars in the frosting as well (the cake in the catalog was dotted with yellow candy sequins), but when I opened the box I found that they were missing. So this is what I did: as Joshua stood beneath the swing set, fishing for something in his pocket, I planted his birthday candles deep in the cake. I pushed them in until each wick was surrounded by only a shallow bracelet of wax. Then I called the children over from the swing set. They came tearing up divots in the grass.

We sang happy birthday as I held a match to the candles.

Joshua closed his eyes.

"Blow out the stars," I said, and his cheeks rounded with air.

That night, after the last of the children had gone home, my wife and I sat outside drinking, each of us wrapped in a separate silence. The city lights were burning, and Joshua was sleeping in his room. A nightjar gave one long trill after another from somewhere above us.

Melissa added an ice cube to her glass, shaking it against the others until it whistled and cracked. I watched a strand of cloud break apart in the sky. The moon that night was bright and full, but after a while it began to seem damaged to me, marked by some small inaccuracy. It took me a moment to realize why this was: against its blank white surface was a square of perfect darkness. The square was without blemish or flaw, no larger than a child's tooth, and I could not tell whether it rested on the moon itself or hovered above it like a cloud. It looked as if a window had been opened clean through the floor of the rock, presenting to view a stretch of empty space. I had never seen such a thing before.

"What *is* that?" I said.

Melissa made a sudden noise, a deep, defeated little *oh.*

"My life is a mess," she said.

Within a week, the object in the night sky had grown perceptibly larger. It would appear at sunset, when the air was dimming to purple, as a faint granular blur, a certain filminess at the high point of the sky, and would remain there through the night. It blotted out the light of passing stars and seemed to travel across the face of the moon, but it did not move. The people of my town were uncertain as to whether the object was spreading or approaching—we could see only that it was getting bigger—and this matter gave rise to much speculation. Gleason the butcher insisted that it wasn't there at all, that it was only an illusion. "It all has to do with the satellites," he said. "They're bending the light from that place like a lens. It just *looks* like something's there." But though his manner was relaxed and he spoke with conviction, he would not look up from his cutting board.

The object was not yet visible during the day, but we could feel it above us as we woke to the sunlight each morning: there was a tension and strain to the air, a shift in its customary balance. When we stepped from our houses to go to work, it was as if we were walking through a new sort of gravity, harder and stronger, not so yielding.

As for Melissa, she spent several weeks pacing the house from room to room. I watched her fall into a deep abstraction. She had cried into her pillow the night of Joshua's birthday, shrinking away from me beneath the blankets. "I just need to sleep," she said, as I sat above her and rested my hand on her side. "Please. Lie down. Stop hovering." I soaked a washcloth for her in the cold water of the bathroom sink, folding it into quarters and leaving it on her night stand in a porcelain bowl.

The next morning, when I found her in the kitchen, she was gathering a coffee filter into a little wet sachet. "Are you feeling better?" I asked.

"I'm fine." She pressed the foot lever of the trash can, and its lid popped open with a rustle of plastic.

"Is it Joshua?"

Melissa stopped short, holding the pouch of coffee in her outstretched hand. "What's wrong with Joshua?" she said. There was a note of concern in her voice.

"He's seven now," I told her. When she didn't respond, I continued with, "You don't look a day older than when we met, honey. You know that, don't you?"

She gave a puff of air through her nose—this was a laugh, but I couldn't tell what she meant to express by it, bitterness or judgment or some kind of easy cheer. "It's not Joshua," she said, and dumped the coffee into the trash can. "But thanks all the same."

It was the beginning of July before she began to ease back into the life of our family. By this time, the object in the sky was large enough to eclipse the full moon. Our friends insisted that they had never been able to see any change in my wife at all, that she had the same style of speaking, the same habits and twists and eccentricities as ever. This was, in a certain sense, true. I noticed the difference chiefly when we were alone together. After we had put Joshua to bed, we would sit with one another in the living room, and when I asked her a question, or when the telephone rang, there was always a certain brittleness to her, a hesitancy of manner that suggested she was hearing the world from across a divide. It was clear to me at such times that she had taken herself elsewhere, that she had constructed a shelter from the wood and clay and stone of her most intimate thoughts and stepped inside, shutting the door. The only question was whether the person I saw tinkering at the window was opening the latches or sealing the cracks.

One Saturday morning, Joshua asked me to take him to the library for a story reading. It was almost noon, and the sun was just beginning to darken at its zenith. Each day, the shadows of our bodies would shrink toward us from the west, vanish briefly in the midday soot, and stretch away into the east, falling off the edge of the world. I wondered sometimes if I would ever see my reflection pooled at my feet again. "Can Bobby come, too?" Joshua asked as I tightened my shoes.

I nodded, pulling the laces up in a series of butterfly loops. "Why don't you run over and get him," I said, and he sprinted off down the hallway.

Melissa was sitting on the front porch steps, and I knelt down beside her as I left. "I'm taking the boys into town," I said. I kissed her cheek and rubbed the base of her neck, felt the cirrus curls of hair there moving back and forth through my fingers.

"Shh." She held a hand out to silence me. "Listen."

The insects had begun to sing, the birds to fall quiet. The air gradually became filled with a peaceful chirring noise.

"What are we listening for?" I whispered.

Melissa bowed her head for a moment, as if she were trying to keep count of something. Then she looked up at me. In answer, and with a sort of weariness about her, she spread her arms open to the world.

Before I stood to leave, she asked me a question: "We're not all that much alike, are we?" she said.

The plaza outside the library was paved with red brick. Dogwood trees were planted in hollows along the perimeter, and benches of distressed metal stood here and there on concrete pads. A member of a local guerrilla theater troupe was delivering a recitation from beneath a streetlamp; she sat behind a wooden desk, her hands folded one atop the other, and spoke as if into a camera. "Where did this object come from?" she said. "What is it, and when will it stop its descent? How did we find ourselves in this place? Where do we go from here? Scientists are baffled. In an interview with this station, Dr. Stephen Mandruzzato, head of the prestigious Horton Institute of Astronomical Studies, had this to say: 'We don't know. We don't know. We just don't know.'" I led Joshua and Bobby Nauman through the heavy dark glass doors of the library, and we took our seats in the Children's Reading Room. The tables were set low to the ground so that my legs pressed flat against the underside, and the air carried that peculiar, sweetened-milk smell of public libraries and elementary schools. Bobby Nauman began to play the Where Am I? game with Joshua. "Where am I?" he would ask, and then he'd warm-and-cold Joshua around the room until Joshua had found him. First he was in a potted plant, then on my shirt collar, then beneath the baffles of an air vent.

After a time, the man who was to read to us moved into place. He said hello to the children, coughed his throat clear, and opened his book to the title page: "Chicken Little," he began.

As he read, the sky grew bright with afternoon. The sun came through the windows in a sheet of fire.

Joshua started the second grade in September. His new teacher mailed us a list of necessary school supplies, which we purchased the week before classes began—pencils and a utility box, glue and facial tissues, a ruler and a notebook and a tray of watercolor paints. On his first day, Melissa shot a photograph of Joshua waving to her from the front door, his backpack wreathed over his shoulder and a lunch sack in his right hand. He stood in the flash of hard white light, then kissed her good-bye and joined Rich and Strange in the car pool.

Autumn passed in its slow, sheltering way, and toward the end of November, Joshua's teacher asked the class to write a short essay describing a community of local animals. The paragraph Joshua wrote was captioned "What Happened to the Birds." We fastened it to the refrigerator with magnets:

> There were many birds here before, but now there gone. Nobody knows where they went. I used to see them in the trees. I fed one at the zoo when I was litle. It was big. The birds went away when no one was looking. The trees are quiet now. They do not move.

All of this was true. As the object in the sky became visible during the daylight—and as, in the tide of several months, it descended over our town—the birds and migrating insects disappeared. I did not notice they were gone, though, nor the muteness with which the sun rose in the morning, nor the stillness of the grass and trees, until I read Joshua's essay.

The world at this time was full of confusion and misgiving and unforeseen changes of heart. One incident that I recall clearly took place in the Main Street Barber Shop on a cold winter Tuesday. I was sitting in a pneumatic chair while Wesson the barber trimmed my hair. A nylon gown was draped over my body to catch the cuttings, and I could smell the peppermint of Wesson's chewing gum. "So how 'bout this weather?" he chuckled, working away at my crown.

Weather gags had been circulating through our offices and barrooms ever since the object—which was as smooth and reflective as obsidian glass, and which the newspapers had designated "the ceiling"—had descended to the level of the cloud base. I gave my usual response, "A little overcast today, wouldn't you say?" and Wesson barked an appreciative laugh.

Wesson was one of those men who had passed his days waiting for the rest of his life to come about. He busied himself with his work, never marrying, and doted on the children of his customers. "Something's bound to happen soon," he would often say at the end of a conversation, and there was a quickness to his eyes that demonstrated his implicit faith in the proposition. When his mother died, this faith seemed to abandon him. He went home each evening to the small house that they had shared, shuffling cards or paging through a magazine until he fell asleep. Though he never failed to laugh when a customer was at hand, the eyes he wore became empty and white, as if some essential fire in them had been spent. His enthusiasm began to seem like desperation. It was only a matter of time.

"How's the pretty lady?" he asked me.

I was watching him in the mirror, which was both parallel to and coextensive with a mirror on the opposite wall. "She hasn't been feeling too well," I said. "But I think she's coming out of it."

"Glad to hear it. Glad to hear it," he said. "And business at the hardware store?"

I told him that business was fine. I was on my lunch break.

The bell on the door handle gave a *tink,* and a current of cold air sent a little eddy of cuttings across the floor. A man we had never seen before leaned into the room. "Have you seen my umbrella?" he said. "I can't find my umbrella, have you seen it?" His voice was too loud—high and sharp, fluttery with worry—and his hands shook with a distinct tremor.

"Can't say that I have," said Wesson. He smiled emptily, showing his teeth, and his fingers tensed around the back of my chair.

There was a sudden feeling of weightlessness to the room.

"*You* wouldn't tell me *anyway,* would you?" said the man. "Jesus," he said. "You people."

Then he took up the ashtray stand and slammed it against the window.

A cloud of gray cinders shot out around him, but the window merely shuddered in its frame. He let the stand fall to the floor and it rolled into a magazine rack. Ash drizzled to the ground. The man brushed a cigarette butt from his jacket. "You people," he said again, and he left through the open glass door.

As I walked home later that afternoon, the scent of barbershop talcum blew from my skin in the winter wind. The plane of the ceiling was stretched across the firmament, covering my town from end to end, and I could see the lights of a thousand streetlamps caught like constellations in its smooth black polish. It occurred to me that if nothing were to change, if the ceiling were simply to hover where it was forever, we might come to forget that it was even there, charting for ourselves a new map of the night sky.

Mitch Nauman was leaving my house when I arrived. We passed on the lawn, and he held up Bobby's knapsack. "He leaves this thing everywhere," he said. "Buses. Your house. The schoolroom. Sometimes I think I should tie it to his belt." Then he cleared his throat. "New haircut? I like it."

"Yeah, it was getting a bit shaggy."

He nodded and made a clicking noise with his tongue. "See you next time," he said, and he vanished through his front door, calling to Bobby to climb down from something.

* * *

By the time the object had fallen as low as the tree spires, we had noticed the acceleration in the wind. In the thin strip of space between the ceiling and the pavement, it narrowed and kindled and collected speed. We could hear it buffeting the walls of our houses at night, and it produced a constant low sigh in the darkness of movie halls. People emerging from their doorways could be seen to brace themselves against the charge and pressure of it. It was as if our entire town were an alley between tall buildings.

I decided one Sunday morning to visit my parents' gravesite: the cemetery in which they were buried would spread with knotgrass every spring, and it was necessary to tend their plot before the weeds grew too thick. The house was still peaceful as I showered and dressed, and I stepped as quietly as I could across the bath mat and the tile floor. I watched the water in the toilet bowl rise and fall as gusts of wind channeled their way through the pipes. Joshua and Melissa were asleep, and the morning sun flashed at the horizon and disappeared.

At the graveyard, a small boy was tossing a tennis ball into the air as his mother swept the dirt from a memorial tablet. He was trying to touch the ceiling with it, and with each successive throw he drew a bit closer, until, at the height of its climb, the ball jarred to one side before it dropped. The cemetery was otherwise empty, its monuments and trees the only material presence.

My parents' graves were clean and spare. With such scarce sunlight, the knotgrass had failed to blossom, and there was little tending for me to do. I combed the plot for leaves and stones and pulled the rose stems from the flower wells. I kneeled at the headstone they shared and unfastened a zipper of moss from it. Sitting there, I imagined for a moment that my parents were living together atop the ceiling: they were walking through a field of high yellow grass, beneath the sun and the sky and the tousled white clouds, and she was bending in her dress to examine a flower, and he was bending beside her, his hand on her waist, and they were unaware that the world beneath them was settling to the ground.

When I got home, Joshua was watching television on the living room sofa, eating a plump yellow doughnut from a paper towel. A dollop of jelly had fallen onto the back of his hand. "Mom left to run an errand," he said.

The television picture fluttered and curved for a moment, sending spits of rain across the screen, then it recrystallized. An aerial transmission tower had collapsed earlier that week—the first of many such fallings in our town—and the quality of our reception had been diminishing ever since.

"I had a dream last night," Joshua said. "I dreamed that I dropped my bear through one of the grates on the sidewalk." He owned a worn-down cotton teddy bear, its seams looped with clear plastic stitches, that he had been given as a toddler. "I tried to catch him, but

I missed. Then I lay down on the ground and stretched out my arm for him. I was reaching through the grate, and when I looked beneath the sidewalk, I could see another part of the city. There were people moving around down there. There were cars and streets and bushes and lights. The sidewalk was some sort of bridge, and in my dream I thought, 'Oh yeah. Now why didn't I remember that?' Then I tried to climb through to get my bear, but I couldn't lift the grate up."

The morning weather forecaster was weeping on the television.

"Do you remember where this place was?" I asked.

"Yeah."

"Maybe down by the bakery?" I had noticed Melissa's car parked there a few times, and I remembered a kid tossing pebbles into the grate.

"That's probably it."

"Want to see if we can find it?"

Joshua pulled at the lobe of his ear for a second, staring into the middle distance. Then he shrugged his shoulders. "Okay," he decided.

I don't know what we expected to discover there. Perhaps I was simply seized by a whim—the desire to be spoken to, the wish to be instructed by a dream. When I was Joshua's age, I dreamed one night that I found a new door in my house, one that opened from my cellar onto the bright, aseptic aisles of a drugstore: I walked through it, and saw a flash of light, and found myself sitting up in bed. For several days after, I felt a quickening of possibility, like the touch of some other geography, whenever I passed by the cellar door. It was as if I'd opened my eyes to the true inward map of the world, projected according to our own beliefs and understandings.

On our way through the town center, Joshua and I waded past a cluster of people squinting into the horizon. There was a place between the post office and the library where the view to the west was occluded by neither hills nor buildings, and crowds often gathered there to watch the distant blue belt of the sky. We shouldered our way through and continued into town.

Joshua stopped outside the Kornblum Bakery, beside a trash basket and a newspaper carrel, where the light from two streetlamps lensed together on the ground. "This is it," he said, and made a gesture indicating the iron grate at our feet. Beneath it we could see the shallow basin of a drainage culvert. It was even and dry, and a few brittle leaves rested inside it.

"Well," I said. There was nothing there. "That's disappointing."

"*Life's* disappointing," said Joshua.

He was borrowing a phrase of his mother's, one that she had taken to using these last few months. Then, as if on cue, he glanced up and a light came into his eyes. "Hey," he said. "There's Mom."

Melissa was sitting behind the plate glass window of a restaurant on the opposite side of the street. I could see Mitch Nauman talking to her from across the table, his face soft and casual. Their hands were cupped together beside the pepper crib, and his shoes stood empty on the carpet. He was stroking her left leg with his right foot, its pad and arch curved around her calf. The image was as clear and exact as a melody.

I took Joshua by the shoulders. "What I want you to do," I said, "is knock on Mom's window. When she looks up, I want you to wave."

And he did exactly that—trotting across the asphalt, tapping a few times on the glass, and waving when Melissa started in her chair. Mitch Nauman let his foot fall to the carpet. Melissa found Joshua through the window. She crooked her head and gave him a tentative little flutter of her fingers. Then she met my eyes. Her hand stilled in the air. Her face seemed to fill suddenly with movement, then just as suddenly to empty—it reminded me of nothing so much as a flock of birds scattering from a lawn. I felt a kick of pain in my chest and called to Joshua from across the street. "Come on, sport," I said. "Let's go home."

It was not long after—early the next morning, before we awoke—that the town water tower collapsed, blasting a river of fresh water down our empty streets. Hankins the grocer, who had witnessed the event, gathered an audience that day to his lunch booth in the coffee shop: "I was driving past the tower when it happened," he said. "Heading in early to work. First I heard a creaking noise, and then I saw the leg posts buckling. Wham!"—he smacked the table with his palms—"So much water! It surged into the side of my car, and I lost control of the wheel. The stream carried me right down the road. I felt like a tiny paper boat." He smiled and held up a finger, then pressed it to the side of a half-empty soda can, tipping it gingerly onto its side. Coca-Cola washed across the table with a hiss of carbonation. We hopped from our seats to avoid the spill.

The rest of the town seemed to follow in a matter of days, falling to the ground beneath the weight of the ceiling. Billboards and streetlamps, chimneys and statues. Church steeples, derricks, and telephone poles. Klaxon rods and restaurant signs. Apartment buildings and energy pylons. Trees released a steady sprinkle of leaves and pine cones, then came timbering to the earth—those that were broad and healthy cleaving straight down the heartwood, those that were thin and pliant bending until they cracked. Maintenance workers installed panels of light along the sidewalk, routing the electricity through underground cables. The ceiling itself proved unassailable. It bruised fists and knuckles. It stripped the teeth from power saws. It broke drill bits. It extinguished flames. One afternoon the television antenna tumbled from my rooftop, landing on the hedges in a zigzag of wire. A chunk of plaster fell across the kitchen table as I was eating dinner that night. I heard a board split in the living room wall the next morning, and then another in the hallway, and then another in the bedroom. It sounded like gunshots detonating in a closed room. Melissa and Joshua were already waiting on the front lawn when I got there. A boy was standing on a heap of rubble across the street playing Atlas, his upraked shoulders supporting the world. A man on a stepladder was pasting a sign to the ceiling: SHOP AT CARSON'S. Melissa pulled her jacket tighter. Joshua took my sleeve. A trough spread open beneath the shingles of our roof, and we watched our house collapse into a mass of brick and mortar.

I was lying on the ground, a tree root pressing into the small of my back, and I shifted slightly to the side. Melissa was lying beside me, and Mitch Nauman beside her. Joshua and Bobby, who had spent much of the day crawling aimlessly about the yard, were asleep now at our feet. The ceiling was no higher than a coffee table, and I could see each pore of my skin reflected in its surface. Above the keening of the wind there was a tiny edge of sound—the hum of the sidewalk lights, steady, electric, and warm.

"Do you ever get the feeling that you're supposed to be someplace else?" said Melissa. She paused for a moment, perfectly still. "It's a kind of sudden dread," she said.

Her voice seemed to hover in the air for a moment.

I had been observing my breath for the last few hours on the polished undersurface of the ceiling: every time I exhaled, a mushroom-shaped fog would cover my reflection, and I found that I could control the size of this fog by adjusting the force and the speed of my breathing. When Melissa asked her question, the first I had heard from her in many days, I gave a sudden puff of air through my nose and two icicle-shaped blossoms appeared. Mitch Nauman whispered something into her ear, but his voice was no more than a murmur, and I could not make out the words. In a surge of emotion that I barely recognized, some strange combination of rivalry and adoration, I took her hand in my own and squeezed it. When nothing happened, I squeezed it again. I brought it to my chest, and I brought it to my mouth, and I kissed it and kneaded it and held it tight.

I was waiting to feel her return my touch, and I felt at that moment, felt with all my heart, that I could wait the whole life of the world for such a thing, until the earth and the sky met and locked and the distance between them closed forever.

Small Degrees

for margie

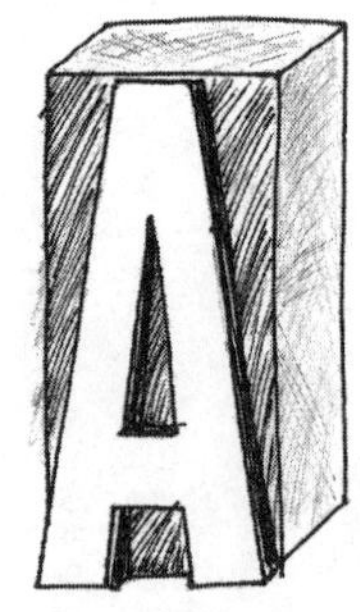

s a small boy he was always sitting cross-legged in the grass, gazing for long hours at this thing or another, an igloo-shape of water in the soil or the brown joints of a stick insect. "A dreamer," his parents said, and they flopped about in their beds at night, for they knew that this would never do. One winter month the whiteness of a blizzard climbed to the second pane of their front window, bottling the world away until spring. He began to study the family books in the glow of the fire. "A scholar," said his father, nodding proudly; and envisioning a desk and leather armchair at the Academy, he went to find his wife. A hopeful few hours later, the boy's mother was dusting in the living room. She asked him a question: "What are you reading now, dear?" and he surprised her by answering, "The letter *n.*" It was then that she noticed him holding his book to the light, staring with perfect emptiness at the blank side of each page. She came to an unpleasant realization. That night she told his father what she had seen. "A fool," she concluded, and his father damply concurred: "A fool."

So when the first adult hairs began to sprout on his chin, they sent him into the city, apprenticing him to the metal founder. A man with a trade, they thought, fool though he may be, was better off than one without. But the boy was not as simple as he seemed. He learned his craft quickly, casting foundry type for printers, raising and reversing each metal word and letter; he had seen such things in shadow before, and he knew their faces and how to distinguish them. He spent his youth and manhood and middle age watching the alphabet roll between paper and plate: sometimes the individual characters became lost, disappearing into swiftness like the leaves of a pinwheel, but occasionally in the turbulence they seemed to distill to a center, boiling apart until he saw the essential glowing wire of their shapes. He met a woman one winter and married her and fathered children, and in time those children grew up, and in time they went away. He worked each day in the orange heat of the foundry and the drumbeat of the presses, walked by the river each evening with his wife, undressed each nightfall, extinguished the lantern, slept by her side, and in this way grew old.

A day came when the type founder was no longer able to cast without pain the copper and lead and antimony of his trade, nor to walk so easily between the foundry and the printing house. Those hands which all his life had been as springy as grasshoppers now trembled after only a few hours' work. The back that had supported him through the many liftings of his children now knew thistles of pain when he rose from a chair. His knees suffered in the cold and rain, and sometimes in the flawless blue days of summer. At least his eyes had never failed him: they were the same eyes that had blinked him awake as a boy. He could measure a stamp to 0.918 inches, number the birds in a V-skein of geese, read a letter or book without tilting his head. So when his body began to unmake itself, he gave himself over to his vision.

These were the days of Edmund and Robert Claire-Mitchell, deans of the Royal School of Type Design, whose spacious roman typeface—inspired, they claimed, by the memory of a shared childhood lover—decorated prayer books and newspapers and bore the name Justina. And the days of Francesco Corie, who developed his influential Plain New Functional design after a twelve-year scientific study of the blinks and eye movements of the proletarian reader. And of Abram Nissen, the inscription sign cutter, whose rich, graceful script carried the dips and serifs of immigrant market signs.

The type founder had been witness to the designs of these men. He himself had cast the plates from which their work was printed. When the first of the Claire-Mitchell brothers passed away at the turn of the decade, he had attended the memorial service, where a muffled drum played and a state dignitary spoke in eulogy. "He gave to our people," said the dignitary, "a system of letters as sturdy and balanced as their own best dreams. The words he made were the words of our shared national dialogue, and his stars were the stars of our flag. We mourn the loss of a great man." The type founder watched the letters of which the dignitary spoke opening and closing on leaflets, undulating on banners, reposing on marble above the new graves, and felt for the first time the wish to design a face of his own.

On a day soon after, he pushed his desk into the light at the east end of his living room. He placed a chisel and brush there, some ink and some lead, and his carving wood and drawing paper. Seven years later, on the morning he retired from the foundry, he took a seat before these tools and began to wait.

* * *

He wanted to design a typeface that would recall his hours of childhood watching: m's and n's and commas that read as fluidly as the swaying of long grass in the wind; b's and d's, p's and q's, like lampposts reflected in a pool of water. He was willing to work gradually, assembling and reexamining each stroke of each character, the hairline of a V or the wedded bowls of a lowercase g, over a period of several days. This may seem a form of calculation, but it was in truth something closer to love, which is to say the reverse of calculation. He was trying to render his heart into letters and signs, and he was a man who discovered his heart only by small degrees.

Sometimes, on her way past his desk, his wife would lean carelessly into him or draw a gray hair from his shoulder. "Working hard, dear?" she would ask, and, "It's coming," he would say. She, for her part, grew lonely during these hours, becoming quiet and inward, and she wondered why he did not notice.

All her life the type founder's wife had risen from bed with the calling of the summer birds or the snapping of the winter ice, to dust and whisk and scrub the house. On Tuesdays she beat the carpets and on Fridays she did the laundry. Then, when her children were still children, she spent her afternoons pottering and wandering about with them, reading to them from a storybook or walking them to the park with the large, blue-brown climbing stone. When they moved on to school and then their own adult families, she had less to fill her time. The high hours of the day became formless and bewildering. By one or two o'clock she would have finished the cleaning; the air would be sweet, the rooms still and empty, and she would have nothing to do. Certain people are skilled in such forms of aloneness: they can take some forlorn thing from inside themselves and shape it into a coin or a bird. But she was not one of them. She passed each free afternoon stirring the fire or pacing the hallway. The little mistakes of her past came to her again and again, and she relived them and shook them from her head. Sometimes she allowed herself to drop into bed for a time and simply lie there breathing. Sometimes she felt in her gut a strange sense of impermanence. She waited for evening and the return of her husband, the clunk of his footsteps on the cobblestone walkway, and she waited for the time when he might spend his days at home.

And now that time had come, and with it had come this new seclusion. He worked some days until his lantern was the brightest thing in the window, and still she paced the hallway, and still she lay sighing on her blankets.

One night she came to a decision. Some short time after she'd withdrawn to their bed, she listened to the sound of him at the washbasin, rinsing his face and scrubbing at his ink-dark fingers. He whipped the water from his hands, then undressed and dimmed the light.

She felt him sitting on the edge of their small mattress. "How far along are you?" she asked.

"I thought you were asleep," he said. He turned back and leaned against the pillows. "Today I worked on the ampersand. It's a difficult one," he said, "so hard to clarify."

"I could just as well not be here, I think. It would make no difference," she said.

"Like trying to tie an elegant knot." He yawned. "What? What did you say? You know that's not true, dear."

What she said next she said calmly and without reservation. She did not raise her voice from a whisper and she did not shift from her side. "Sometimes I try to talk to you when you're working. I'll need to hear another voice. And when you twist your head to look at me, or when you wave me away for a time with your finger, I can see that it's as if I've vanished into some other moment. You think that people are nothing but time," she said. "You think that I'm nothing but time. But I'm not time," she said. "I'm something else."

What was he to say to such a thing? If he was this sort of person, he had never recognized it: he wasn't sure he even knew what it would *mean* to recognize it. As he tried to puzzle it through, he heard her breathing deepen. A cricket sounded at the window, and the house and all its spaces seemed to spread with an electrostatic silence. "I don't know," he said. "Perhaps you're right." And when she didn't reply, he closed his eyes and gathered the blankets to his shoulders.

He was soon asleep.

The next morning there was an answer waiting for him on his desk, written in his wife's hand: *I love you,* it read, but the word *love* had been crossed out and replaced with the word *miss,* which had been crossed out and replaced with an empty space, as though his wife had given up on the message altogether.

He looked for her in the kitchen and the pantry and the bedroom, though he'd just come from there. He stood on the front walk and watched his neighbors drifting by like sails: she was not among them. He even tapped on the trapdoor of the attic with a broomstick, querying her name with a brief little note of embarrassment in his voice. When it became clear that he was alone in the house—and because the day was supposed to begin in this way—he lit the stove and drew the curtains and prepared a breakfast of eggs and toast. He completed the stem of a k that morning, and busied himself that afternoon with the initial stroke of a W. All day long he listened for the sound of her shoes in the hallway, their change from pad to click at the edge of the carpet and floor. He listened for the snap of wood as she spurred the fire, and the creak of the pantry door on its hinges, and the thousand peripheral noises that told him he was home and she was near.

It was not until the sun fell that he realized she had left him.

* * *

The type founder had kept house only rarely in his life—and then just for the few short days it took his wife to mend from a sickness or return from a visit to the children's—and the orderliness he'd known for years on end seemed to give way over succeeding weeks to a slow confusion of dirt. The stove filled with heaps of white ash, and dust collected at the saddles of doorways. A gray-green discoloration on the bedroom window sill fattened from a dot to a blotch to a bell-shaped stain. When he walked across the carpet in the sunlight, he could see transparent cloudlets erupting from beneath his feet, and when the temperature dipped in the evening, he heard popping and groaning noises inside the walls. It was as if the basic matter of his house, the board and the tile and the stone, was separating joint from joint. The process seemed beyond his control. He fell to his work.

As he leaned over his desk each day, lead or brush in hand, his head would fill with scenes that were charged with the vibrancy of memory. Sometimes he simply watched these scenes—allowing them to sharpen and dim or to mist away into other memories—but often a particular image would grow so rich in its detail that he could not help but moisten his brush and spread before himself a few leaves of paper, compelled to represent it. He began each picture with a jot of black ink and pursued its strokes and bends to the corner of the page. The drawings he made were not very good, and he knew this, but occasionally he would find in them some small piece of a letter that would make all his efforts worthwhile. He discovered in a sketch of a streambed the polliwog tail of a capital Q. He found the crook of a j in the upturned beak of a sparrow, and a question mark twist in the shadow of a door knocker. He saw these things suddenly, with a start in his breath like the lashing of a whip, and he struggled to perfect them with his brush and his hands. He fell asleep sitting at his desk, awakening in the morning from dreams of stone tools and cave art, of dyes made from blackberries and paintbrushes chewed from the fiber of twigs. His fingers tightened into a fist, and he massaged them with mint oil. His face became feverish, and he covered it with a wet cloth. When the elements of a letter had all taken shape, he drew a final copy of it on a sheet of china clay paper. He carved it, reversing the structure, into the end grain of a hardwood block. And he set this block in a case of shallow drawers, ready to be pressed into molds at the foundry—to be cast into type of a more durable sort.

Sometimes, when the letters lay hidden and he had to search his memory, a vision would come to him of the bruise-colored stain at his bedroom window. It was an image like a snare, holding his thoughts close and tight, and to see his way past it was like the tussling of an animal.

It was a sky-blue spring morning when the type founder carved the finishing stroke of his final letter: a capital I. He blew the shavings of wood from his desk and watched them float into the air. Then he went to wash his hands in the basin. When he came back, the line of the sun had moved from the edge of his desk to the carpet, casting his type case in a haze of black shadow. He repositioned the case in the light against a wall and stepped back to take a look. Its cells were filled, its hinges glinting—A through Z and a through z in roman and italic, all the marks of punctuation and all the marks of reference.

Every character was complete, filed neatly in its drawer, and he drew a satisfied breath, feeling as new of heart as a flourish of wedding confetti. That afternoon, he thought, he would button himself into his vest and jacket, fasten the clasps of his type case, and carry it to the foundry. It wouldn't take long to produce a plaster mold, and afterward to cast his work in lead and in antimony. He might walk home as early as nightfall, his arms heavy with metal type. Then he would prepare a stew for himself, with meat from the butcher and greens from the grocer, and he would hold the letters in his hand as he ate, testing the heft of them one by one, their satisfying coolness and the fineness of their grooves.

As these words went rolling through him, the type founder followed the slant of the sun across his storage case. And though it took him a moment, he noticed something there that brought his thinking to a halt.

The light moving over the rows of type had pulled at the darkness and glare of the letters: certain hollows had grown deeper, certain angles had grown sharper, certain flags and descenders now shone as white as day. The image they formed in their turns of light and shadow became clearer as he squinted away the details. It was the face of a woman, her head cast slightly to one side. A strand of hair fell over her cheek, and she was staring as if into a great distance. It was like the shape of a cloud in an oncoming rainstorm, both distinct and illusory, and he recognized that it was nothing more than a product of his own dreaming vision. All the same, he would have watched it until evening struck, but a short time later a flock of birds disrupted the sunlight. The image rippled in their passing and then vanished from his sight.

When he left his house that afternoon, he thought that he was setting out for the foundry. His jacket and vest were buttoned close and his type case was swinging in his hands. But at the corner by the large blue-brown climbing stone, where the road into town met the road to the river, his feet remembered a different path.

He found himself standing alongside the water, first beneath a walnut tree and then on the bank where he used to walk with his wife. A couple of children were marking the soil with long sticks, and an old man nearby stooped to inspect the cuff of his pants. A butterfly floated along the shoreline with its otherwordly wings. It was only when the type founder saw a mother lifting her baby from a carriage, heard her pat the space between his shoulders with a "hush-a" and a "there, there," that he realized his mistake: it had something to do with aspiration, and neglect, and the river that was flowing past him, and the choice to walk there unaccompanied, and he felt his own foolishness rise up inside him and send a frost through his body.

Then, sick with the weight of his thoughts, he shaped that foolishness into a wish, cupped that wish for a moment in his hand, and sailed it into the water like a stone.

And who's to say that such gestures are without consequence, that our hopes and petitions can have no influence in this world? The type founder knew as if it were the clearest of his memories what he would see when he got home and opened his front door. He set his type case against a tree—it was finished now, and he no longer needed it—and he started up the riverbank. Then, thinking better of it, he turned back and gave the case to the woman who was coddling her baby. "Alphabet blocks," he explained, "for the child."

He made his way along the cobbles as swiftly as he could, and arrived at his porch with the sting of the walk still burning in his lungs.

His wife was in the living room, her back to him, running her finger through a line of dirt at the window: it was just as he had wished it, just as he had seen it. He opened his mouth to speak and his throat made a rustling noise. "Sometimes—" he began, and she turned to look at him from the window. He stood in the open doorway and a small wind slipped around him. *Sometimes we have the wrong dreams,* he was going to finish. *I'm sorry,* he was going to say. But his wife gave a little smile, a freshet of red in her cheeks, and rubbed the dirt from her hands with her blouse.

"I know," she said, nodding. "I know." She gestured around the room, where currents of dust were swirling in the spring air. "We've got some work to do here, don't we?" she asked, and the look on her face was a sign that welcomed him home.

The Jesus Stories

And there are also many other things which Jesus did, the which, if they should be written every one, I suppose that even the world itself could not contain the books that should be written.—John 21:25

This is one story: Jesus, the son of Mary, born by law into the house of Joseph and by custom into the line of David, but whose true father, the Holy Spirit, was engendered of no one, went out into the world to find his people. In the hills beyond Jerusalem he met Satan, who said to him, "I am Man's Prince, and you are Man's Son, and we are of a kind, you and I. These stones can be as bread to us. These cities can be as beds. Everything you see here is your home." But Jesus answered him, "You are not of my family," and departed from him into Galilee. There he gathered around him twelve disciples, and he lived with them for many years, telling them stories and supposing them to be his brothers. But they did not understand him, for they were not of his family, so in time he sent them away. He was called to a wedding in Cana one day, where he met his mother. Seeing her, he was filled with sorrow, for though she embraced him as a son, even she did not truly know him. She was of this world, and he was of another. "Woman," he said, "what have I to do with you?" When he died on the cross, he died between strangers.

This is another story: At Golgotha, the place of skulls, Jesus was crucified, and wrapped in linen, and sealed into the earth, and this might have been the end of him, but it was not. It is given to each of us to experience everything. This is God's secret, the invisible truth that gives shape to our lives: everything we are capable of knowing, feeling, and suffering, we will. Jesus, being God, was capable of infinite experience, and so he returned to this world, every part of him, to finish living his life. His anger caused the earth to shake and ripped the veil of the temple. His joy sent a clean wind whistling through the trees. His sorrow went walking through empty rooms, smothering candles and moaning like a spirit. His body appeared to his disciples on the road to Emmaus, and their eyes were opened, and they knew it to be him. And though his body was carried into heaven, the rest of him—the anger, the sorrow, the joy—remained behind. Every ghost story is another chapter of the Gospels.

The N. are a religious people, converted to the Christian faith by early Jesuit missionaries; they are steadfast in their commitment to the church, if unorthodox in their application of its creeds. It is the purpose of this report to provide a brief account of the conversion of the N. and to examine the key artifact of their culture: the pleocanonical Gospels, or, as they are more popularly known, the Jesus Stories. I have spent the last five years studying these texts, and while I have not yet finished my review of them, I believe that I am in a position to submit my preliminary findings.

First, I shall briefly discuss the conversion. Tradition tells that when the Jesuit missionaries first appeared to the N., gliding from out of the sunlight beneath an array of white sails, the people mistook their ship for a giant bird, and were astonished when it gave up to the sea a host of tiny men. A tribal document describes this first encounter: "The men rowed ashore and spoke to us in a strange tongue. They came clothed in heavy robes, which they would not remove, even though the heat of the sun was upon us. They wore crosses on lines around their necks. 'What place have you traveled from?' we asked them, and they answered, 'God has sent us to you,' a phrase which sounded like a riddle or a proverb in our tongue[1] and so made us laugh."

We know that the missionaries stayed with the N. for many months, as long as three years, introducing them to the customs of the church. "They gave us wine to drink, and read to us from a book they carried. They sprinkled our heads with water they collected in coconut shells." The missionaries slowly learned the N. language, and in time they were able to participate with the N. in their storytelling ceremony, the central ritual of the tribe. Every evening, after the sun had dropped, the people would gather around the common fire and exchange stories—true stories and legends, folk tales and fantasies, the saga of Bird and Lizard, the romance of the sun and the moon. Ten or twelve of the N. would speak each night, taking privileged seats within the ring of stones, and when the final voice had

[1] A direct translation would be: "A blueness resides in the monkey."

gone silent, the teller of the best story would extinguish the common fire and the N. would sit in the coal-light and ponder his tale.

The stories the missionaries told were new to the N., and the N., it is reported, were shocked to discover that the missionaries actually believed them. From a tribal document: "They told us about Noah and the parade of animals. They told us about Joshua commanding the sun to stand still. They told us about Jonah and the whale, Elijah who would not die, Jesus arising from his tomb and flying. We were solemn when they finished. The insects were loud in the trees."

Within a year, schoolbooks inform us, the N. were all Christians.

The things I describe happened long ago, of course. N. is a modern country now, a nation of the world, with glass buildings and highways and libraries, just like our own. Though the people still perform a version of the storytelling ceremony during the four seasonal holidays, it is only a shadow version, enacted when their families gather around the table to eat. A candle or a lantern replaces the common fire, and the youngest member of each family is permitted to blow out the flame and make a wish. In this and other ways, the N. honor their heritage. They fast once a year, on the day the sea turtles climb ashore to mate, and on the day their eggs hatch, digging their way up through the sand, they feast. They hold a festival of kites each spring to remember the missionaries who sailed to their land (as the annual Kite Day speech declares) "like a bird from out of the sunlight." And on their thirty-third birthday, for a month or a year, they take a sabbatical from their jobs and families to write their stories of the life of Jesus.

It is these stories—the Jesus Stories—which are the central achievement of the N. culture. They are regarded as a treasure by church scholars and anthropologists, and are kept bound and cataloged in the Gospel Archives of the N. National Library. I have read over 14,000 of them in the progress of my research, and I can testify to both their great pinwheeling surface variety and their deeper unity of vision.

Many of the stories take as their genesis incidents described in the accounts of Matthew, Mark, Luke, and John. Christ's forty days in the wilderness is a popular point of commencement, with the dual attraction of his fasting and his temptation. There are stories that relate his dialogue with Satan, that depict his hunger visions and the weakening of his body, and one which hints that he in fact died in the wilderness and only then became revealed to himself as God. Various stories concentrate on his castigation of the Pharisees, his healing of the sick, his burial and resurrection, his grief on the Mount of Olives. There are new treatments of each of his miracles and parables, lending to them a thousand different shades and nuances. One story takes as the defining episode of Jesus's life the killing of the children of Bethlehem precipitated by his birth—an incident that the story designates "the slaying of the ten thousand," recalling perhaps the song of the women of Israel: "Saul has slain his thousands, and David his tens of thousands." It suggests that the record of the days of Christ (and, subsequently, of Christianity) is one of blood and suffering, that the slaughter of the children of Bethlehem left a mark on Jesus's life that could not be erased. It provides a detailed account of the crucifixion, lasting several pages, and also describes the subsequent torture of the apostles. It concludes with a litany of the deaths of the saints. The final line is one of the most famous in N. literature: "Spare us, O Lord, the pain of your turning away."

Another story inspired by the same incident tells of a Bethlehem schoolteacher who spends two years in an empty school building waiting for her next class of children to come of age. Called the Teacher's Story, it was written only a decade ago and became hugely popular among the N. A mass-market printing by a major publisher spent upwards of thirty weeks on the national best-seller list.

It is not unusual for the more visionary of the Jesus Stories to take their own places within the Biblical tradition of the N., adding to Christian mythology and touching off new stories, not unlike the Gnostic Gospels of Saint Thomas and Mary Magdalene. The Story of the Slaying, for instance—mentioned above—is widely believed to be the source material for the Teacher's Story: both depict characters found nowhere else in the Gospel accounts (Thaniel the merchant; the angry Samaritan) and both make use of the same epigraph, from Matthew 3:10: "And now also the axe is laid unto the root of the trees." Another example, perhaps more telling, is that of the Young Man Stories. In the early years of this century, a tailor from the coast of N. wrote an account of the life of Jesus that centered on the young man who followed him when he was taken by the soldiers at Gethsemane, an incident mentioned briefly, and exclusively, in the Gospel of Mark.[2] The story presents the young man as an angel of the Lord, at hand to witness the fulfillment of the prophecies. A second tale, written a few years later, gives the young man a more robust role in the drama, as an angel who is present at Gethsemane to *release* Christ, should he ask, from his duties as the Messiah. This story opened the floodgates. Later versions depict the young man as a thirteenth apostle, as one of Christ's brothers, as his adopted son by Mary Magdalene. The most recent addition to the Young Man Stories suggests that he was Christ himself, traveling during the days of his burial to revisit the events of his life. This story grafts the young man like a bud onto the

[2] Mark 14:51–52: "And there followed him a certain young man, having a linen cloth cast about his naked body; and the young men laid hold on him: and he left the linen cloth and fled from them naked." See also Mark 16:5.

central episodes of the Gospels, and it takes as its main token the linen cloth that he wore at Gethsemane, suggesting that this was the selfsame cloth that Jesus later (earlier?) cast off in his tomb.

Though many of the N.'s stories attempt to elaborate upon incidents mentioned in the Scriptures, others more closely resemble the folk tales and fantasies of the early storytelling ceremonies. Most of these tales take place between Jesus's twelfth birthday and his immersion at the age of thirty in the river Jordan, a span of years for which there is no record in the Bible. One, for instance, tells of Christ's journey to the Americas, where he lives with the native inhabitants and develops into his manhood. Another tells of his transformation into a bear by the demons of Hell, who, though they cannot destroy him, are able in this way to conceal him from himself: in this story, Jesus wanders as a bear for many years, "bedding in the caves, eating of the trees and streams," before he sees his reflection in the eye of a dove and remembers who he is. Another story tells of his descent into the Great Sea to deliver his teachings to what the text calls "the people of the water," or "the people of the ocean." A hero tale in the classical tradition, it presents Jesus as a man of adventure, favored by God, who helps the people of the water do battle with the beast Leviathan. Upon his leaving, the people furnish him with an amulet that will give him power over the water and the creatures of the sea: "We give you this gift, O Man of Earth, so that you might summon the fish from their hiding pools, and multiply them for food; so that you might still the tempests, and calm the waters, and walk with ease upon them." Certainly the members of the N. who first listened to the testimony of the Jesuits were struck by the fantastic—and often miraculous—nature of their accounts, for many of the earliest of the Jesus Stories are built on just such fantastical transformations as this.

It would be impossible in this preliminary report to provide a comprehensive record of the writings of the N., for their literature presents to the reader a boundless variety of stories, as inexhaustible as the imagination of mankind, which is the imagination of God. The following, then, is only a small sampling of the Gospel Archives' most recent acquisitions:

A story that depicts Jesus as a man of great solitude, given to silence and isolation, who hides himself from us in mountains and deserts, who speaks to us only in puzzles, who weeps plainly at any daily sight. The story has a refrain, "See that no man know it," which Jesus says after each parable and to all those he has healed. Though God loved us and wished to redeem us, the story suggests, he suffered greatly in our company.

A story that portrays the Lord as a builder of houses. The first of his houses, which he names Adam, he builds on a foundation of sand: "And the rains descended, and the floods came, and it fell: and great was the fall of it." The second of his houses, which he names Jesus, he builds on a foundation of rock (i.e., the church): "And the rains came, and the winds blew and beat upon that house, and it fell not."

A story that presents a series of dreams about Jesus, each belonging to a different apostle, or to another of the figures from the Gospels—Lazarus, Pilate, Simon the Cyrenian. The most interesting of these dreams is that of Judas Iscariot, who imagines himself as an insect climbing the body of

Christ, unknowingly stinging him with his poison, in order to place a crown upon his head. Each chapter ends with the same verse: "And he awoke and knew that it was holy, for the dreams of men belong to God."

A story that consists of only one word: Yea.[3]

A horror story, based on Matthew 27:52–53, in which the graves are opened and the bodies of the saints walk into the holy city. For three days, between the hour of Jesus's death and the hour of his resurrection, the saints wander the streets of Jerusalem, heavy on their feet, walking blankly into houses and market stalls, massing at sundown on the temple steps. When the stone is rolled from Christ's tomb, they collapse into piles of dead men's bones.

A story that emphasizes as the first message of the Gospels the value of forgiveness. This story also sees many of the parables of Jesus enacted in his own life. In analogy with the parable of the two debtors, for instance, Jesus forgives the debts, both monetary and spiritual, of all his apostles, and Peter, who owed him most, loves him best. In analogy with the parable of the friend at midnight, Bartholomew the apostle appears at Jesus's door one night while he is sleeping, and though Jesus tries to stop his ears to his friend, the knocking persists, so he arises and lets him in.

---

[3] Matthew 5:37: "But let your communication be, Yea, yea; Nay, nay: for whatsoever is more than these cometh of evil."

A story that depicts the fever dreams of Jesus as he hangs on the cross. Jesus imagines that he has forsaken the path of his calling to live a life of human pleasures, that he has wed and founded a home outside Jerusalem, that he is a contented old man surrounded by the generations of his family. At the end of the dream, he awakens in great suffering and rejoices.

A story which suggests that God became flesh not just to redeem us, but also to understand us, "the most bewildering of all His creations." To redeem us he became Christ, who contained in himself all that was righteous and pure, but to understand us he became Judas, the betrayer, whom the story describes as "the most frightful sight of his time" and a man "unvisited by any virtue." The drama of Christ's last days, then, is presented as a contest between these two aspects of God—between God who wishes to save us and God who wishes to know us.

A story which proposes that Christ has *already* returned, that he transported his elect to heaven shortly after the resurrection and that the rest of us are living, without understanding, in the epilogue of human history. The story presents the entire record of the modern era as a single strand of the Tribulation: "Verily I say unto you, This generation shall not pass away, till all these things be fulfilled."

The literary quality of these stories varies greatly, as do the theological principles that inform them. They seem to speak to both sides of every moral issue, and they subscribe to no one set political or economic doctrine. For every story that champions socialism ("Make not my Father's house a house of merchandise"), another story champions wealth ("For unto every one that hath shall be given: but from him that hath not shall be taken away even that which he hath"), and another story champions ambiguity ("Render therefore unto Caesar the things which are Caesar's; and unto God the things that are God's"). At first glance, in fact, the Jesus Stories may seem merely a hodgepodge of ideas, as formless and contradictory as the motions of birds in a storm, hopelessly irreconcilable with one another and with church tradition—and indeed, the N. have often been misunderstood. They have been charged with violating the decree of Saint John, who wrote in Revelation 22:18: "If any man shall add unto these things, God shall add unto him the plagues that are written in this book." They have been denounced for lacking piety. They have been mistaken for heretics, atheists, and antinomians by church leaders.

The N. do not seem concerned by these accusations. I asked my good friend J., curator of the Gospel Archives, who has been so helpful to me in the five years of my research, for his stance on this dispute. He smiled and spoke for his people when he said, "Just like you, we are trying to understand."[4] Indeed, I believe this to be true. The stories of the N., examined with generosity, enrich our tradition rather than

---

[4] J. recently showed me the story he himself composed in his thirty-third year. Every culture, he says, tells the tale of a man who finds himself lost in a fog in his home city, where the thickness in the air makes everything look unfamiliar. He takes shelter in a store he has never seen before, a store that is full of wonders, with a beautiful shopkeeper at the desk, and walks home after the fog has cleared. The next day, he returns to the same street to give the shopkeeper his thanks. But try as he might, he cannot locate the store. The neighbors tell him that it burned down years ago, or that it closed its doors when the shopkeeper died, or that it never existed at all. The man spends the rest of his days looking for it. According to J., the fact that this tale

unraveling it. They show us new ways to imagine that most cherished of human events, the life of the Word made Flesh. Jesus himself, after all, spoke to us in parables.

One last thing remains to be disclosed in this report: the final purpose, one might even say the ambition, of the Jesus Stories. The N. believe that it is our duty as Christians to tell *every possible story* of the life of Jesus, and that each of us must make a contribution to this project. This is how they interpret Christ's counsel to "Go into the world and tell what you have seen": an instruction to the faithful to consider the Scriptures and make them new. It is not without significance, they maintain, that this instruction is followed immediately in the Gospels by Christ's promise to return. When the final story has been told—the N. believe—when all the possibilities have been exhausted, Jesus will descend from the heavens and the Kingdom of God will be upon us.

---

is so widespread suggests its basic importance. It must speak to something that we all understand. J's story, then, presents the story of the life of Jesus in this light: he stumbled into this world in a fog, and found it lovely, and has been trying to find his way back ever since.

Space

A tall white candlestick burns beside me, its wick an orange comma in the pivot of its flame. The light fades into darkness by slow degrees, and beyond it I see almost nothing—not the stiles of the fence, not the spines of nearby rooftops, not power lines roping to the ground, only headlights swaying on far roadways and barbed white stars hovering in the sky. It is as if the city itself has wandered into sleep, fastening its lids over windows and streetlamps and neon signs. The candle flame slants in the breeze with a muffled flutter, the sound of an old filmstrip as its tail slips from the

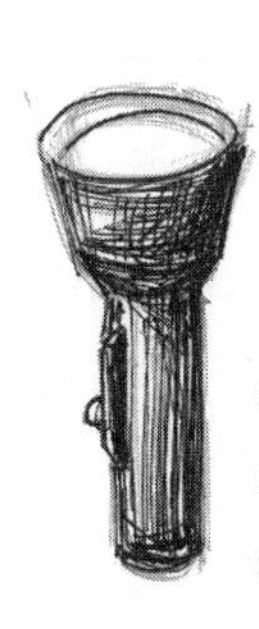

projector. Eric, our son, reaches to settle it, then presses a finger to the rim of his wristwatch. He crooks his arm, exposing the lucent blue pool of a facedial. "Two hours," he complains, filling each word with his breath. He reclines into the straps of his porch chair. There is the light of the stars, the light of the candle, and between them the steady arctic glow of his watch—dimmer than the others, less hungry, more remote.

The katydids are bounding from thin blades of crescent grass. The stars are wavering in the sky.

Two hours ago I lay in the bathtub, submerging my hands in the bubbles and watching them poke like little buoys to the surface. The water dimpled at my chest each time they rose, then flattened again as they fell. I was searching for a word—what is it?—the name of that force which holds a curve of water above the lip of a glass?—when the lights went out with a soft abrupt tick. As I stood and reached blindly for the towel rod, I could hear the bathwater trickling from my body into the tub, though I could not hear much else: not the refrigerator humming in the kitchen, the mutter and throb of the television, the sigh of cool air through the ceiling vents, the purr of electricity behind our floorboards and carpets and walls. Fastening the towel around my waist, I stepped from the bathroom and into the hallway, where the ceiling fan was languishing to a halt.

In the living room, Eric sat in an armchair before the blank face of the television, pecking at the buttons of a remote control. *Damn,* he kept whispering. *Damn. Damn. Damn.*

"What happened?" I asked.

He tapped once more at the keypad of the remote before placing it on a table. I heard sipping, swallowing, the click of ice cubes in a glass. "Power's down," he said.

"Where?" I said. "Just here?"

"How should I know?" He bit into an ice cube, punctuating the thought. "Look outside."

Standing in the doorway, I gazed out at the stars. They were everywhere, dangling from the arm of the Milky Way in dense silver clusters and floating at the far rim of the sky. The moon was invisible—couched, perhaps, behind trees and high buildings, or hidden in the earth's shadow—and the lights of the city had been entirely extinguished. I looked from one star to the next: each seemed to flare brighter and larger, dilating like a bud into flower. A broad-winged katydid gave a whirry leap onto the screen of a nearby window, and the night air resounded with a rich lyric chirring. I couldn't have told you which I was listening to, the voice of the katydids or the voice of the stars. You would have loved this sound, Della.

Now I sit on the back porch, my hands knit together in my lap, and a low breeze rustles through the grass. A narrow gold band is looped around my ring finger, and inside it the candle flame describes a filament of sharp white light. I draw in the scent of the grass and the dark summer soil.

"Either the main wire is down," Eric says, "or there was an overload at the power station." He brushes his fingers along his jawline, scratching at a patch of stubble.

A satellite sweeps through the Northern Cross. I monitor the sky for shooting stars.

"Weather seems fine," I say.

Eric stifles a yawn as he answers. "Maybe somebody fell into the generator," he says, touching his lips. "Some bum or something." I listen for a whiff of laughter, but there is nothing.

"Maybe," I say. Is this what I should say? "But probably not."

* * *

Three months ago, Della, the city lay hidden beneath a jacket of snow. A flat glacial light was gathered inside the trees and billboards and houses, and heavy clouds slumbered in the gray air. At your funeral, a man with wire-rim spectacles and a black cassock recited a series of verses: Matthew 28:20, John 3:16, Genesis 49:33. The glare of a suspended lamp shone from his lenses, transforming his eyes into vacant white plates. He spoke in a voice like the rustling of leaves, and when he was finished he cleared his throat with a cough. He stepped from the rostrum. He fingered his cross. We filed past you in mute farewell.

In the vestibule, voices hummed and whispered in my ears, and slow willowy hands brushed my arm and my shoulder. I could feel the weight and stillness of the cool quiet space beneath the ceiling. I could see the dim mosaic of the high windows. Our son stood in a side doorway, his head bowed, his chest and stomach giving a few rough heaves. He pressed his hand to his eyes, blotting them dry, then gazed at his fingers. He watched them as if they had returned suddenly from somewhere far away. When I found myself at his side, meeting his eyes through the gaps between his fingers, I did not know what to say.

"She would—" I began. "She was very—" But I couldn't finish.

He touched my coat sleeve and told me not to worry.

In the car he rested his temple against the window, and his breath made little clouds on the glass. I wondered whether he was watching this, or the flow of the asphalt, or his own reflection. Sleet and snow thaw coated the roadway: arcs of it spurted from beneath spinning tires, spattered from lane to lane, and burst; a spine of it, gone gray with exhaust, wound down the center of the road between the streams of traffic. Eric unhitched his seat belt, and its blue sash drew taut beside him. "Are you all right?" I asked. My breath hovered for a few white seconds in the car, then thinned and passed.

"I'm okay," he said, his voice slow and milky. When I placed my hand on his shoulder, he jerked—involuntarily, it seemed to me—and drew away.

"You know, Eric, if you need to—"

And suddenly he was yelling at me: "Didn't I tell you I would be okay? Didn't I *just* say that?" He gathered his breath into a long sigh, then said, "Please, Dad. Please. Can't we just stop poking at it for a little while?" Above the houses and the thin, swooping power lines, a flock of birds dropped silently into the arms of a single bare oak tree. They seemed like a sudden, dense foliage, and as they lifted again I thought of autumn leaves snapping their bulbs and whirling into the sky. "If that's what you want," I said. "I won't say another word."

That night I woke from an oppressive dream. Our bedroom was thick with silence, thick with shadows. I decided to pour myself a glass of water. In the hallway, a cord of light shone from beneath Eric's door. I could hear him behind it: he was sobbing convulsively, gulping for air, and I rested my hand on his doorjamb. A slat of white light covered my socks. "Eric?" I said. He didn't answer. As I stood in the dark—feeling my heart bat in its cage, wondering if he had heard me—he slowly seemed to comfort himself. The spasms of his voice began to ease, and his breathing began to soften. The silence over the next few minutes grew, broken only now and again by a quick, constricted pant. I listened, and brooded, and cared, but I found myself unable to knock.

In the kitchen, water dribbled from a silver faucet into the sink. The glow of a streetlight hazed in through the window. I stood there wondering what I should have done, my nightshirt lifting with each breath.

Outside, the streetlight flickered above the snow. A strong wind piped between the trees, rattling through their dry, weblike branches. It had blown the sky clear while I slept, and I could see the stars pulsing in the night and the eye of the moon rising far above the earth.

* * *

The candle flame shifts from side to side like a flower petal spun between two fingers. It is yellow from peak to tail and black at its focus, with a horseshoe curve of blue dwindling along its sides. Peering into the dark central pinch of flame, I can see an image of Eric's shoulder and the rim of his chair. When I turn to him, he is leaning in on himself, plucking at his lower lip and staring into the grass. A machine or an animal is making a knocking noise somewhere. It sounds like a woodpecker hammering holes into a tree, louder than the katydids, louder than the cars. Do you remember the day we heard the woodpecker rapping on the oak tree by our driveway, Della? It was our first morning in this house together, our first morning away from the city, and neither of us recognized the sound: you thought it was somebody pounding nails into a board, and I thought it was somebody banging on the front door. Do you remember what you said when our next-door neighbor told us what it really was? You said, "If we have to have holes in our trees, I guess there might as well be birds nesting in them." I think about this all the time.

"Jesus," Eric says. "That's one noisy damned bird."

"I doubt it's a bird. Woodpeckers aren't nocturnal."

"Whatever it is, I feel like it's knocking inside my own head." He mimes firing a shot from a rifle. "What I wouldn't give for a gun right now."

A katydid springs into the candlelight, landing on a yellow dandelion head.

"Your mother—" I say, and Eric twitches up, leaning toward me. I can feel something inside him—someplace dense and wary and hidden—becoming white-hot with brief attention, but it falters before I can speak. "When she was a little girl," I say, "she kept a flashlight by her bed. She told me that she would stand by her window and point it into the sky at night. She would find a spot without stars and shine it there until she went to sleep. She thought that the light would reach a planet one day, someplace without a sun. The people there wouldn't be able to see where they were going and suddenly—light. She wanted to help. She told me that."

Wisps of grass cast twitching black shadows in the candlelight. "Where?" asks Eric.

"What?"

"Where? Where were you when she told you that?"

The punctilio of a headlamp swerves at the horizon. I can't remember.

"It's been a long time," I say. "I'm sorry. I can't remember."

"Right," says Eric, loosing another broad yawn. "Okay," he says. Then he turns away, pinches to a center, draws in on himself like a tight, snarled knot.

I am afraid, Della, that as I climb from the well of this time into days of habit and quiet persistence, into weekends and birthdays and sudden new seasons, the things that I know of you will slip quietly away from me. I am afraid that as the glass of my life falls away, I will forget you, and what I believed of you, and what I loved of you. I will sit on the porch steps one brisk fall morning, watching the scissoring legs of the dawn joggers, listening to the warble and peck of the birds, and I will try to call you to mind, and I will fail. I will walk into the living room and find that your face has become just a photograph on the mantel, your name a signature on a yellowed envelope. I will sweep my fingers along the hallway walls and feel them skip against a lappet in the wallpaper, and I will sit at the foot of my bed and gaze into the carpet. I will not remember the timbre of your voice or the cast of your body. I will not remember the breadth and measure of your stride. I will not remember the hunch of your shoulders as you walked against the wind or the set of your elbows as you knotted a scarf. One smoky winter day you sat in an armchair and leaned into the heat swell of the fire, unbuckling the buckles of your boots, and afterward you stood with a foot raised to the hearthstone, drew back the mesh of the fire-screen, and spurred the fire, then settled in beside me as the sparks raged white and yellow up the chimney—it's a small thing, Della, but this too I will not remember. I will not remember the disposition of your mind and heart toward myself or the world or any one thing. I will forget it all, everything that matters. The arc of your laughter, the contour of your face, the tuck of your lip as you arrested a yawn. The treble-drum rhythm of your hand and wrist—one-two, pause, three—as you rapped on a door or sounded a car horn. I will forget that you browsed at corner newsstands and answered jingling pay phones, that you counted during storms the seconds between lightning flash and thunder crack, that you held our son to your chest and let him cry the day a circus clown fuzzed him with blue confetti. The manner in which I knew you, the moment of our acquaintance, whether you were gracious or severe, soulful or sharp, hopeful or frail with regret: all these things I will not remember.

What I will remember is this: That there was a Della. That in a place now gone dark, within some vale or crimp of lost time, I knew her. And that something of her life passed into and through my own, effecting a conversion. My memory of you will be like the envelope of a bubble—rising out of sight from the collar of its wand, transporting the breath of me to some far place.

My memory of you, Della, will be like the last, quiet pulse of an echo: were I to follow it, I could not say what towards.

I took our son last week—but you know this—to see the fireworks. From the shelf of a low hill, we watched people stroll from the car park and settle in beside us. Families clustered around ice chests and blankets, around collapsible chairs and grills with glowing coals. Wiry adolescents threw frisbees and packed-foam footballs. As night fell, the heat that billowed from the ground made a chain of lens-shaped clouds over the lake. The first two fireworks were launched from their cannons with a deep, bass *whoompf,* erupting above us in showers of red and white. The next one descended in shimmering blue scarves, and another sprayed out from its axis like the leaves of a green palm tree.

Eric sat beside me, teasing a blade of grass into dozens of separate fibers. "I keep thinking," he said, "about that time when the spark almost hit me."

For the first time in weeks he was volunteering to talk, and I almost couldn't believe it. I swallowed before I spoke. "I'm surprised you remember that," I said. "You couldn't have been older than three or four."

"I do, though," he said. He let the grass fall to the ground. "You were holding me on your shoulders. We were watching the fireworks and something went wrong with one of them."

"It exploded too soon."

"Right. What I remember is the sparks. They were raining down into the trees and the lake, and then one must have caught the wind. It fell right beside us. When I looked down, the grass was on fire."

"Just a tuft," I said. I smiled and found myself laughing. "You screamed so loud, my ears were ringing for hours."

"I *know,*" said Eric. His lips spread into a thin smile. "I was terrified. I didn't calm down until you poured your drink on the fire."

"I remember," I said. The grass had been brown and withered, and the fire had gone out with a sound like the flurry of a cymbal. "That wasn't me, though, actually. With the soda. It was a man with a ball cap and a mustache. I didn't know him."

"Oh," said Eric, and his voice died a little. He lifted a finger to his temple. "Strange that I thought it was you." A firework leaped from the shaft of a cannon with a lurid shriek, and he gave a start. A shiver snaked its way along his shoulders. The sky shone green for a moment—I could see it flashing from his cheek—and behind us a small girl began to clap.

Eric pressed a hand to his chest. "Where was Mom?" he asked after a moment. "When the grass caught fire."

"She was sitting on top of the ice chest," I said. "The spark couldn't have fallen more than a few feet behind her, but she didn't notice. When I tried to tell her about it afterward, she wouldn't believe me. You had fallen asleep by the time we packed the car, and she carried you home in her lap."

"Hmm." Eric eased himself into the grass and propped his head on his wrist. A firework burst above us, and I watched its flares reflect from the surface of the lake, cascading through the water like a school of luminescent fish. Another shattered into sharp blue lines that gleamed from the bellies of two low clouds.

"It looks like lightning," Eric said. He lay gazing into the night, his free hand twisting the wing of his shirt. "What do you call it—you know—the kind that doesn't strike ground."

"Search me," I said.

"We've been studying it in science class." He closed his eyes for a minute. "Cloud-to-cloud. That's it. There's cloud-to-cloud and cloud-to-ground."

"What's the difference?"

I could see him frowning in the yellow light of a firework. "What do *you* think, Dad?" he said. "Cloud-to-ground is the kind that sets trees and houses on fire. You know, that zigzag shape. Cloud-to-cloud is just a flash in the sky."

"Interesting," I said.

He sighed. "To you it's interesting. To me it's just work. Do we really have to talk about science class?"

"We can talk about anything you want."

"Good," he said. "What I want is not to talk at all. Can we do that?" He lifted himself onto his elbows. "Let's just watch the explosions for a while."

It is a week later now, and all the lights are out. Eric sits in his porch chair and pivots his head to follow something above me—the wind or the stars or the stray smoke of some inward vision. An expression slips into his eyes, timid and wistful, like a fish or a turtle come to surface in a well. "Forty-eight," he says, skittering a hand through his hair.

I turn toward him. "Forty-eight?" I ask.

"The katydids," he says. "You count the times they shrill in twenty seconds: forty-eight. Then you add thirty-nine and it gives you the temperature." He taps his finger on his wrist, calculating. "Which would be eighty-seven, I think."

"Like lightning," I say, trying to listen. "You count the seconds between the lightning and thunder, then divide by five. That's how far away it is." The candlestick burns quietly above a pool of setting wax. I am speaking for a moment as if I were elsewhere, without weight, form, or presence. "The lightning," I say. "In miles," I say. "Your mom taught me that." Then I attempt a joke: "But you don't like to talk about lightning, do you? I forget."

Eric shuts his eyes. He doesn't laugh, but I can tell he is listening. "Dad?" he says.

"Yeah?"

He twiddles at the ruptured plastic tag of his shoelace, then scratches his cheek.

A moment later he says it again: "Dad?"

"What is it, Eric?"

It is then that the power flickers on. We notice it first from a distance. All of a sudden we can see the shape of the city on the land: all the streetlamps and buildings and windows. It is as if the earth and the sky are reaching into one another, exchanging their lights, like clasped hands interthreading fingers. I can hear a rattling sound coming from the air conditioner, and from the living room the voice of a television commercial: *Isn't it time you considered training for a career as a medical assistant*? "Yes!" says Eric, and he hops to his feet and claps his hands. I have not seen such a clear display of emotion from him in months. "Thank you, God!" he says. "Finally!" A light from inside the house sends the shadow of his body slanting in a long line over the lawn. Then, just as suddenly as it returned, the current shuts down and the million lights of the city vanish. The fan in the air conditioner whirs to a slow stop.

I shrug and clap my leg. "Looks like a false alarm."

Eric gives a soft *goddamnit.* "I am so sick of all this," he says. He sits down again, shifting in his chair, and the candlestick hides his face from my view.

"Eric?" I prompt.

"Why can't I just watch TV?" he snaps. "Is that too much to ask?" He leans forward and jerks his head, then punches himself in the arm, a tiny thudding sound muffled by his shirt. It rises in me—the instinct to say "Don't hit yourself"—but I know better. He would squeeze shut like a snare. Instead I ask, "Are you okay?" and he gives a strangled laugh.

"I'm okay when I don't have to think about it," he says.

"I know," I say. "God, I know. Sometimes I wake up at night, and I feel—peaceful. I feel peaceful, and so I think that it must not have happened yet. Isn't that crazy?"

"Not crazy." He shakes his head. "The same thing happened to me the first few weeks, but then it stopped all of a sudden. It won't last forever." He sighs. "But to tell you the truth, I liked it better before it stopped. I just want something to be easy for a change."

One star, more brilliant than all the others, hangs like an ornament at the horizon, swelling brighter and then dimming, swelling brighter and then dimming.

"And it's easy to watch TV?" I say.

"It's easy to watch TV," he agrees.

The katydids are out there calling their names.

The tiny red light of an airplane passes through the sky. It soars past a low cloud, the North Star, the bold white W of Cassiopeia—vanishing and reappearing, winking in a long ellipsis. Inside, its passengers read glossy periodicals, summon stewardesses, and unbuckle their seat belts. They gaze from the panes of double windows and float away in a tight red arc.

"Two hours, twenty minutes," says Eric, illuminating his watch face. He stretches and gives a deep yawn, then throws back his head, tightens his lips, and another shudders through him like a ripple through a pond. "Look, I'm going to turn in," he says, standing. "Nothing to do out here anyway." He excavates a particle of dirt from beneath his thumbnail.

I watch him tuck his hands into the big loose bowls of his pockets—they swallow him up to the forearms—and dig soil from the lawn with the toe of his boot. After a while, he stops short.

"Well," he says, and his chin gives a little jerk. "Good night."

"Good night," I respond.

He steps to the door and it whispers open. Do you need the candle? I think. Can you see your way? But the door slides shut behind him.

A cicada is perched at the edge of the porch, shrilling its drums and fanning its wings, mirroring the candle in its small black eyes. The wind is hissing through the grass and the stars are guttering in the sky. Sometimes, Della, it feels as if I am living inside a mirage. Sometimes it feels as if I myself am the illusion—a wavering in the air, an apparition in a weave of bodies. The pulse of your flashlight is thirty years gone. Such a long time it's been sailing past moons and planets, past stars and dark matter and stray comets. It's been coursing through the gulf of space, its beam like a long silver road. It passed Alpha Centauri as you dressed for your first dance, Sirius as you left home for college. It passed the faint white globe of Tau Ceti as you lifted your veil and braided your fingers through mine.

It's going, Della. It's on its way.

One fine day, it will burst through the sky of a black world, flashing from trees and houses and lakes. Doorknobs and fenceposts will cast thin sharp shadows. Turtles will poke from their shells, and bears will stumble from the mouths of caves. Men and women will throw open their windows, trembling and blinking as they step through their doors. On that day there will be banquets and celebrations. The people will dress in their finest robes. The feast will be grand, the conversation merry, and everyone will watch the sky. How I wish you and I could be there as well.

The Passenger

I was just a passenger, and like all passengers, fundamentally unconcerned with landscape and plot, enveloped only by the simple movement of it all, the cumulate graph of those coherent points where we ate, slept, went to the bathroom, and awaited movement again.
—Scott Bradfield

And I've got the sun in the morning
I get the cold every night
If I had to do it all again
I'd have been born in flight.
—Bill Morrissey

My mother gave birth without benefit of midwife, bed gown, or epidural anesthesia, and with the added discomfort of a safety belt firmly secured across the dome of her midriff. My newborn body, dangling umbilically above a pool of broken water, floating for a moment between one fact and another, found itself then drawing breath—discrete, unanchored, and folded to her shoulder. By this window she released me into the world, and seated here I have spent my days. When my mother died, I was left her empty seat and her carry-on luggage—quiet condolences, moist, extended hands, and the fevered conviction that she was just waiting in line for the toilet. When my mother died, they put her in the sky. She fell limply through the air, through a pass between the clouds and toward the green. She had asked that it be so. *When I die,* she told me, *let me go—let me wing my way straight to the ground.* From this window, I watched her scarf flapping red, straining to loose itself from around her neck. It swam like an arm against the drop. She tumbled out of sight.

All of this was long ago. Before I lost my mother, I had been given to speculation. Was there a place for us outside the confines of this cabin—how would the human body comport itself in the sky? Would it fall, I wondered, and if so, which way: into the clouds or into the stars? Or would it take up position where you left it, grow steadfast in the air, a buoy above the passing clouds and a perch for chirping birds? Like a nail puncturing the wall of space, like the fossil of a whisper, would it simply, faithfully, hang there? My mother opted for descent. Perhaps it's all a matter of appetite.

If you were to seat yourself along the trailing edge of the port wing—your shoelaces dangling over eight miles of wind and air and a sensation as of something small and heavy (a stone, a clock, a paperweight) falling through the hollows of your legs—and if you were to look from this place to the left and then up, you would see a window and behind it me. I might wave hello. I might tell you of the things I've seen, the fleeting images of blue and white that emerge from beyond my window and are lost somewhere behind me.

Familiar and forgiving, they sometimes afford me a sense of contentment. If I spoke, though, you couldn't hear me. You would sit there shrugging your shoulders. It is early afternoon—and will be for quite some time, since our path today approximates that of the sun—and beneath me the shadow of our vessel slips like a length of limp rope over valleys and ridges and frothy, anviled crests of cloud. When darkness falls, I will press my cheek against the window and look up. I will see glancing streaks of meteor and the moon's hollow eyes. I will see the stars and their implicate white hunger. Sometimes there are stars beneath the clouds as well, sometimes nothing but a rolling blackness.

Across the aisle from me, two old men are sleeping, snoring with open mouths, their heads resting on thin gray pillows and their seatbacks fully reclined (as fully, that is, as circumstances allow—as fully as a back-bent thumb, or the leg of a capital *A*). Elsewhere, people napping next to windows have drawn shut the flimsy plastic shades, as thin as a pane of dried paint, that wobble when we hit a belt of turbulence and produce a sound not unlike the thrum of fingers across an ashtray lid, and not unlike swallowing. Some of us, sleeping, cover our eyes with thick nylon visors. We receive these every few weeks, pouched together with a set of twilled gray socks, a pinky-sized toothbrush, and a tube of grainy mint toothpaste. No one wears the socks. One of the men across the aisle hasn't shaven in what must be weeks. His sideburns stretch across his cheeks, silver and frizzled, and he mutters in his sleep, something about investment securities. The man beside him breathes through his lips and scratches at the prominence of his chin. A few of us read airline periodicals. A few look out windows. Ruddy-faced men wearing print ties and starched white shirts roll their sleeves to the elbow and stare at the lambent screens of laptop computers, typing vaguely, enigmatically.

A wide-screen television overspreads the front wall of our cabin. Six others crane down from above the aisles. Together, they resemble the legs of some overgrown plastic insect stuck fast through the roof of our plane, its antennae juddering in the wind. The televisions are a jumble of films and documentaries and airless situation comedies. The woman who lives ahead of me is listening to them through her headphones. This is all I can see of her—these headphones and the dark swoop of hair pinned atop her head. A few errant locks drape themselves over the back of her seat. They are like ropes from a church tower. If I pulled one, it would set bells ringing. She could call me Quasimodo.

* * *

Our craft arose from a world of balloons, developing gradually into the vehicle we now ride through a fortuitous and baffling series of evolutionary advances. Though direct evidence of the earliest of these advances is scant, our scientists continue their research—rifling through luggage, prying sheetrock from the walls, and peering keenly through convex lenses into seat pockets, sink drains, and the sediment of ashtrays. They scribble equations onto their notepads in the belief that by examining closely the world in which we find ourselves, they can determine the path along which we've traveled. The process is analogous to following with one's eye the path of a contrail as it recedes into the distance (although no analogy is exact: contrails tend to peter out too quickly for close study and aren't, I'm told, scientific enough).

Our forebears—after a complicated series of random events within, first, a hostile atmosphere of hydrogen, methane, ammonia, and water vapor; then a life-supporting cushion of oxygen, carbon dioxide, and nitrogen; and finally a primordial soup of carbohydrates, nucleic acids, proteins, wicker, and fat—found themselves suspended in a swaying wickerwork gallery beneath the envelope of a hydrogen-filled linen balloon. Buffeted relentlessly by heaving winds, they had little control of their craft and even less shelter. They drifted through the pipe and wail of the sky, through a tangle of clouds and sharp wind. Our ancestors knew none of the comforts of modern life—not cushioned chairs or thermostatic regulation, foil-wrapped peanuts or tumbledown television shows. Life was ugly and brutish and often quite chilly. Hour after hour, they would stare into the changing clouds—a repose of shallow haze, an unfolding of cauliflower blooms—and into the frail pleated shell of their balloon.

Utilizing an aluminum framework, our predecessors constructed the dirigible—which, steam-driven and rigged with bags of lifting gas, saw them steering their way through the sky. Next came the powered glider with its lightweight gasoline engine and its stubby, wire-braced wings, which were overspread by the fabric of the now-lapsed balloon. Soon thereafter followed the all-metal monoplane, the DC-3 (streamlined, piston-engined, variable-pitch-propellered), and the jet aircraft in which—but for a few minor adjustments for the sake of comfort and convenience—we now ride. Most of these final developments have been realized within living memory: a new in-flight magazine appears every month, a new television roster biweekly, and peanuts with ginger ale approximately every two hours—but no one can recall the all-embracing evolution of our vessel from one thing into something wholly other. Days go by, people age, children are born, and very little seems to change.

Most of us believe either the conjectures of the scientists—who rest the weight of their authority upon a firm foundation of past accomplishments, among them the discovery of the constant speed of light, of the constant speed of matter, and of levity, that force which separates all objects from each other and keeps us balanced here between the earth and the stars—or the conjectures of the clergy.

"Ye shall be as stewards above the earth," reads the Book, "over man and over fowl and over every flying thing that flyeth through the skies." Our stewardesses, contend the clergy, citing as evidence this and other verses, function as something akin to a surrogate God. Stewardesses, they say, are representatives of the divine will, enacting sacred rituals and preserving the hallowed order. Through the antennae of their silverpoint fillings, of their numinous and cycling breath, they receive the pulse of messages from a higher plane of existence. The stewardesses will neither confirm nor deny these claims. They ignore our hymns and oblations and our fitful sectarian squabbles. They aren't taking questions. Though civil enough—I've yet to see a stewardess strike a child, say, or expectorate in public—they are often aloof. From beneath a veneer of natty buttoned uniforms and thin hazy eyes they project a hint of menace, and just a suggestion of scales. When a believer, his hands damply clasped in prayer, approaches a stewardess and asks of her a sign, a token display of dew or wind or fire, she will offer him an antiseptic smile, a pillow, and a bag of peanuts and direct him firmly to his seat. Still, faith persists.

Central to our theology is the contention that God is steering our course, that we're not simply wending along the trail of some ancient wrong turn, straying without purpose through the multitude of clouds, wandering here in seclusion; that we've aim and that we've bearing; that we're traveling with regard to destination. God, our theists propose, is capably and majestically engaged in a sequence of sacred and arcane transactions—maintaining altitudes, monitoring radarscopes, guiding trajectories, pitches, and rolls. He is heedful of our needs and of our hushed, sunken wishes. Long ago, He spoke with the voice of a thunderclap, addressing our ancestors from thin air, and the intercommunication speakers curling like halos above each seat represent the conviction that He will soon break His millennial silence, extending a golden invitation of voice to His faithful. The occasional believer claims to have heard the ripple and crackle of speech sounding from these devices, but such claims, we have learned, are of dubious authenticity. The button by the intercom, when pressed, evokes only an anxious wheeze of static. Some profess that God's guiding hand once manifested itself as well in the back-and-forth play of the mandates posted throughout our vessel—that in the days of our grandparents' grandparents these mandates were signs of His will, lit or extinguished as a measure of divine vexation. No longer. Now, were the signs demanding that we refrain from smoking and fasten our seat belts quenched, we would sob and rend our garments, beat our breasts and wring our hands. Shivering and biting our nails, we would wait for the flames and the sudden, angular convulsions.

Although tensions were once the rule between theology and science, they have diminished in recent years. Our clergy and our scientists both search the gridwork of our travels for a set of present coordinates, and on this path they have each discovered the other. On this same path I have found myself, drifting through the world without holiness or reason—a pinch between remembered and anticipated time.

The wings of a plane appear separate, self-contained, and unattached, but are actually all of one piece, passing through the plane's body and under the feet of its passengers.

* * *

When children are born, the fuselage fills with the scent of human. The bankers order cocktails, the Malthusians mutter of population density, the voyeurs peek across aisles and over seat tops. The barbers knot their bow ties and croon lullabies in groups of four. The accountants huzzah, the cartographers smile, and the tobacconists hand out cigars. When children are born, the stewardesses barrel down the aisles, wheeling carriages fraught with fruit juice and ginger ale and vest-pocket bottles of liquor, asking that we return to our seats, please, immediately, and extinguish all smoking materials. When children are born, their carry-on luggage is found resting securely in the overhead compartments.

Our children enter this world bearing their futures in the form of oblong leather suitcases, green canvas duffel bags, zip-and-hasp purses, and multiform other containers, their luggage tags empty of address and destination. The contents of these vessels often imply the path that a child will travel—anticipating hobbies and humors, predilections and professions—and the moment when a newborn's luggage is first opened is met with unease and much stirring of the heart by his parents. A child with an erector set will likely be an engineer; with a telescope an astronomer or geographer; with a text on the merits of the Library of Congress versus the Dewey Decimal System a librarian. A child born with a powdered wig will likely be a magistrate, with a stethoscope a doctor, with a whiskey flask a lost and splintered soul. From time to time, a child is found with stores of illicit substances sealed in plastic pouches or small glass vials within jars of ground coffee. These children, our stewardesses tell us, will be placed in remand when we reach the proper authorities—a threat that rings hollow, it would seem, for more often than not such children come of age, marry, and entertain highly successful careers as politicians or wealthy gadabouts. Folklore tells of a child who arrived here with a liberal supply of gelignite, detonating caps, duct tape, and inflammatory leaflets. He was ejected from the plane, they say, and his paraphernalia with him. Those who tell this story speak also of wily pretended innocence, of ducks and snakes who drown in lakes, and of resident natures, inborn streaks of character, that we can't suppress and can't evade.

My possessions are as follows: three black ballpoint pens, a ream of narrow-ruled notebook paper, several paperback novels, a thesaurus, an electric razor, a wallet and a walletful of business cards and folded bills and photographs of smiling people I don't know, a heavy woolen blanket, a pair of socks—one with a snarl of loose thread in the toe—and a pair of cotton briefs, several cassette tapes and a portable cassette player without batteries, a roll of peppermint lozenges, two packs of chewing gum, and the clothes on my back, and on my front, and on my sides. Also: a nervous reserve, a repressed libido, a wandering pain, an overindulgent imagination, a distaste for the word *basically,* a keen memory, a flawed but burgeoning sense of aesthetics, an affinity for balloons, three facial tissues—as coarse as parchment—plucked from the washroom and folded in my pocket, a song that I don't know pulsing steadily in my ears (it begins *Button, button, who's got the button*—that's all I remember), a memory perhaps not so keen after all, a history of dreams with blatant lingering symbols, a cold sore, two hangnails, and on some days not a friend in the world.

This craft is a lesson in social gradation, a traveling structure of class distinction. Life here comes in strata. The wealthy reside in first class—privy, I'm told, to multifold luxuries: palatable meals replete with frozen gourmet desserts, stimulating periodicals, daily sponge baths, and access to a masseur, a masseuse, and a sauna. The rest of us sit sequestered from the privileged few before the quill and gather of thick maroon curtains, one in either aisle, behind which, if you listen carefully, you can hear the festal, immaculate sounds of good fortune: quiet conversations, the ting of fine silver, and shameless and manifest snoring. I, like most, live in coach. I dine on a bland lettuce-bed cuisine. I have my own window and a measure of solitude (a rare thing, this, but my mother's seat has been left empty since she went her falling way), and I consider myself fortunate. I could be closer to the washroom—this I admit—but not without being forced to abide the jostle of hips and elbows, the nods and curt hellos of waiting strangers. I am pleased with my position in society. The disadvantaged and the dispossessed reside within the underbelly of our ship—coughing, uncounted, in cargo. Though we know they exist, we rarely see them. Sometimes we hear the clamor of a scuffle, on occasion the recurrent bass rumble and spluttering drum of an upswelling personal stereo. Once I heard somebody shouting about somebody else's clothesline.

On holidays, the wealthy march through our aisles on their way to cargo, bearing as gifts food stamps, bottles of brandy, and gleaming silver trays laden with baby potatoes and redolent, dressed turkeys. They claim, when asked for donations, that they don't support charity or handouts, they don't support something for nothing. *Give a man a fish,* they say, *and you feed him for a day, teach a man to fish and you feed him for a lifetime* (an expression I have never understood, though I suspect what it means is this: *Throw a man overboard, and you don't have to feed him at all*). Still, they always come back from cargo empty-handed.

* * *

My mother used to tell me this story: once, she would say, long before you were born, the world was nothing but cloud. Nimbostratus and cumulonimbus. Stratocumulus and altostratus. Lengthy rolling cords of cloud spun one about the other. Isles and wheels and braids of cloud billowed and drifted through space. A wadwork of clouds bottled earth and breath and ocean, corking everything, sealing it in, and the world looked from a distance like a swollen mass of cotton.

Into this hold of vapor there flew a plane. *The plane,* my mother would say, *in which you're sitting here beside me, the very plane in which I'm telling you this story.* This plane had soared through many galaxies, passing flights of strange and wondrous things as it traveled, and as it flew across the reach of space, weaving and dipping past moons and stars and planets, it left behind it a trail of condensation—protracted, white, and, it must be noted, very much resembling a filament of cloud.

Now, as the airplane approached this world of ours, the clouds grew curious. For the first time in the history of all things cloud, a stranger neared: not a comet, not the moon, but one of their own. This was *a cloud,* they could see—a cloud that had crossed the interstellar medium, with baffling courage and otherworldly vigor, bearing at its head what appeared to be a drop of mercury. Heaven only knew its port of exit. Heaven only knew its port of call.

The approaching cloud was flying quickly, and it might, the clouds realized, pass them by, so with their gusty voices, they called to him. *Hey,* they cried, and *here,* they cried, but to no avail. The thread of cloud unreeled itself nearer—and with a sudden shifting tone flew past. The clouds, puzzled, knit their brows, and the sky went rippling away.

It may be, suggested a voice, *that we're out of earshot.*

Or perhaps, said another, *that bead of mercury has lodged itself in his ear.*

The other clouds thought this a splendid hypothesis, for squall as they might, the thread of cloud simply hastened away.

Clouds are almost nothing in the sky, just drops of condensation riding the wind, but things of breath and water can be quite resourceful when the times demand. And so, gathered one and all, a concurrence of clouds, stratus and cirrus and altocumulus, concocted a plan. So that the passing stranger might hear them, they would pluck the bead of mercury from his ear.

From the brawniest of thunderheads to the smallest wisps of haze, the clouds began to coalesce, swelling and sluicing and splashing about one another. They curled and foamed into a vast grasping hand and then heaved themselves higher into space, growing thinner and thinner as they reached away.

Just as the airplane was sailing out of reach, two fingers of cloud—index and thumb—plucked it from its course, and a palm of cloud crooked around it and drew it along the wire of its wrist toward home. When the clouds again dispersed, they found matters not at all as they had left them. For unwittingly, as they had drawn away—past the winds, past the moon, and through the void—they had uncorked the bottle in which was kept the world: the blue-green, vertical ocean. The trees and the fields and the mountains. The ripe, breathing land and all the lights scattered across it.

And the ball of mercury the clouds had carried home was not a ball of mercury at all. It was, it seemed, alive.

And so, my mother would tell me, the airplane on which we ride, and in which your head is resting on my lap, circles this planet, leaving behind it a streak of cloud—and since cloud is one thing and earth another, fated to remain distinct, we soar here over the fields and the oceans, waiting for the day when we might land. The clouds have become just a part of this world, melting above it in the sky. The condensation trail—hanging like a blur across the lens of night—has dispersed, but never quite vanished, becoming what we call the Milky Way. And the world, my child—the sunken, wayward, rolling world—is but a misunderstanding of vapors.

My mother would tell me this story often, when the sun had crept from out of the sky. My head in her lap, I would gaze at the ceiling, listening to her voice and waiting to fall asleep.

* * *

The woman who lives in front of me, the one with the black hair that drapes itself over the crest of her chair; the woman whose face (eyes, cheek, turn of lip) I can't recall; the woman whose face, when I see it, seems to bypass my eyes altogether, drawing itself into focus like an image hidden inside me all along; whose fingers rise from the nape of her neck and drift through her hair like upswept wisps of smoke; this woman, who sends my heart blowing through me like a bomb—I believe that she's bearing my child.

I'm not sure. It happened four months ago, and we haven't spoken since. When she passes by, I turn my head as if I'm looking out the window. I watch the ailerons lift and subside as the plane banks into the wind. I watch our shadow flit and gutter over the clouds. When she sees me coming, she feigns sleep. I won't rest my feet in the bay beneath her chair, and she won't recline for fear of touching me. We are like children who wrap their hands over their eyes and believe that the world has gone blind, as if we both wanted this, and I don't know why. She never hurt me, I never hurt her. We just don't talk.

It was happenstance, a chance event, an up and a down in a clear blue sky. The sun hovered overhead, blazing from its apex and blinking like a star from the wing. We were flying through the first lashings of a fit of wind shear. Wind shear, as a rule, is no menace. Its effects are modest—the quick shiver of cutlery on a tray table, perhaps, or the flutter of an overhead light. On rare occasions, someone standing in an aisle will stumble and steady himself against an armrest. This was different, though. The doors of yawning luggage compartments fell shut in a series of heavy whoompfs. Loose window shades slid down their chamfers. A sound like metal striking metal came from somewhere underneath the plane, and luggage caromed noisily above us, slamming from wall to wall and rupturing zippers and buckles in a muffled white explosion of socks. When the wings began to pendulate (throwing the passengers to the floor and the ceiling, slinging the fuselage around like a rubber ball fastened to a paddle), she was walking past. I turned my head.

She staggered from seat to seat in the aisle—once, twice—without moving forward. I could feel at this point the jog and back-sling of my body against the seat belt. I could hear her drawing breath, a series of rapid hiccups. She slipped then, and in a glissade of pebbly limbs she fell into the chair beside me. "Are you all right?" I asked. She nodded. The pupils of her eyes were like two tadpoles skittering nervously through standing water. She held her right hand pressed to her heart.

I could call someone, I thought to say—but as the first syllable rose from my throat, her torso fell rigidly, sharply forward. She tucked her head between her knees. "Hello?" I said. My finger grazed the ridgeline of her back.

Across the aisle, a tray table swung down from its cove and, striking level, shuddered on its hinges (ours—I checked—were secured behind their latches).

"You should buckle up," I said. No response. The cabin was still reeling, and each time it rose she skipped slowly forward in her chair. Reaching over her, I grasped the pin frame of her seat belt. I threaded it through the hollow of her body—which, collapsed upon itself, resembled the thick maroon curtain at the head of our cabin that had fallen seconds before in a heap to the floor—and I buckled her in. With the back of my hand, I could feel tiny, quick breaths budding in her abdomen. The turbulence subsided.

I waited with my hands clasped in my lap, and soon she lifted her head—sitting upright and breathing calmly, slowly, through her nose. Her eyes were closed. Just before she opened them, both of her brows flexed gently downward, and a ripple of thin muscles passed over her eyelids. I had never noticed such a thing before. She looked at the seat belt fastened across her lap, and then, quizzically, at me. "Sorry," I said.

I heard the faint pop—like a bead of water striking the sink—of her lips as they disjoined. "No matter," she said, and she unbuckled herself, standing as if to leave.

"Wait," I said.

"What?" she said.

"So where were you going," I asked, "before?" (This is precisely the sort of thing I find myself saying if I'm not careful.)

"I was thinking," she said, "that I ought to find a place to sit down." She sat down. "It's never been this bad before—has it? The turbulence, I mean."

And then, from the blue, we were talking.

She said she was a tribologist—she studied interacting surfaces in relative motion. We discussed wing drag and crosswinds and friction. We discussed many things, as shafts of windowed light kicked toward the ceiling, and she touched, once, the bay of my neck.

A stewardess, happening by, addressed us in a voice murky with suspicion. Would we, she asked, like to make any duty-free purchases—a carton of cigarettes, perhaps, despite long-standing proscriptions against open flames and smoking itself, or a matching set of stuffed bears, aviator and aviatrix, with soft brown fluff and bomber jackets? Since we were now leaving international waters, she explained, this could be our last opportunity. My partner declined for the both of us, and the stewardess reluctantly left. Her lips were pressed together like thin white loaves, and her head swiveled to watch us as she walked away.

Later, when the woman yawned, shivered, and her pupils, in the shade of some deep and private vision, dilated, I asked her if she would like a blanket. Without a weight of this sort, some heaviness to lie beneath, I sleep with unpleasant dreams—I'm floating away, turning to spirit, untenanting my body, unhappening my history. I kept, at that time, a thick woolen blanket under the seat, and I spread it over her lap and across my own. With lowered eyes we settled in beneath it, and I don't think it surprised either one of us when I found her hand folding over my knee, or when she found mine cupped at her stomach, or when hers drew up and mine drew down, and there came an ungathering, an unbuckling, an unravelment and extrication.

It culminated with her skirt collected at her waist, my trousers at my knees, and—so as not to disclose anything to the stewardesses—the blanket covering the both of us (though I thought this a practical solution at the time, I've grown suspect; we were probably about as hush-hush as a pair of loosed flares). I remember two things: the rasp of the seat cushion against my skin and the pucker and slow deflation of the sun at the horizon.

That evening she slept with her head on my lap, and I with mine on her back. When I woke, the western sky was a deep violet behind our plane. The first stars were glimmering ahead, whistling their light from across the universe. I stood up, laying her head on a pillow, and left to wait in line for the washroom. When I returned, the pillow lay tucked atop a heap of blanket, rumpled and unattended. She sat sleeping in her regular seat, directly in front of me. Her temple and fingertips converged unconsciously upon an armrest, and I stood above her from behind. Watching her features in quiet seclusion, her unstirring lips and calm, closed eyes, I decided it best not to wake her.

* * *

When the body is inactive (during sleep or rest or untold hours spent idling in a chair) the fluids in its joints thicken and swell, producing a suspension of glairy threads that come to resemble the gel within a grape. My life is testimony to this. Sometimes my legs are like shafts of cast iron, fused and bolted at the knees; sometimes my spine is a sickled thing, bowing sharply forward; sometimes my ankles spread fibrous, tangled roots through my feet and into the floor, and they coil and sprout around spars and trusses, branching away beneath the cabin. When I stand, it sounds like marbles dropping in the washroom. I stroll the aisles of our cabin when I can, working my stagnant muscles, often ducking into vacant seats to avoid oncoming stewardesses.

The features of our vessel—the seatscape and the aislescape, the windows, the walls, and the people—are long established and well recognized. Very little changes. Turning left as I leave my seat, I approach the anterior of our craft and the rimpled maroon curtain bounding us from the first-class cabin. Along either edge of the aisle, a transparent rubber capillary, in the bore of which runs a string of tiny lightbulbs, delineates the walkway. In times of emergency—power failures, blown fuses—these lights have proven themselves helpful. I used to be able to watch them for hours, tiny bulbs blinking dimly on and off, as my head dangled over the lip of my seat and my legs stretched up its backrest. I have always been fascinated by things like this, by holding patterns, spiral rolls, events that loop in on themselves in a seemingly endless fashion, like the play of the moon across the sky, or the unceasing flow of water from a broken faucet.

An older couple, married, sits beneath the wide-scope television screen at the front of our cabin. Often when I pass them they are playing cards, pasteboard aces, knaves, and nines fanned across the face of their trays. Blackjack, poker, gin rummy. The husband has been ill—I can hear him breathing, a heavy, rustling wheeze, from my seat above the wing—and soon, walking past, I'll see his wife playing patience. Elsewhere a man reads a limp-covered novel and pulls thoughtfully on the crook of his lower lip. Two women complete a crossword puzzle in erasable ink. A small boy with sprangled ears and a tuft of leaning hair harasses his older sister, creeping his hand like a spider over the seat cushions until it is poised at her pants leg and, when she notices, retrieving it by means of the other, which picks it up and runs to his lap. The girl soon complains to her father, seated behind them, who yawns and, with an unconvincing glare of disapproval, tells his son to stop the foolishness and stay on his side of the seat. Yawning is a widespread phenomenon here. People yawn, others see them yawning and, in turn, yawn themselves, still others see the second-order yawners yawning, and so on—until a single yawn, like a scattering ripple, has spread itself throughout the fuselage, and our collective radius of hearing has tripled. The passengers in first-class never yawn at all. Reports suggest that each of them is furnished with a fresh supply of oxygen, stored in large metal canisters with snaking, transparent outlet hoses and shell-shaped rubber face masks.

The line outside the washroom is often staggered and unruly, stretching halfway through the cabin. Those who've reached the front wear haggard and uneasy faces. They stare guardedly at the sign wheeling between VACANT and OCCUPIED above the doorknob, and their fingers thread through their hair, as matted and tousled as rain clouds gnarled by the wind. Returning to my seat, I pass a woman who, shifting and shrinking, attempts to extricate herself from beneath a lowered tray table without upsetting the edifice of food and beverages on top. With a sudden wresting of her hips she prevails. Then—standing atop her toes in the aisle, opening the overhead compartment—she retrieves a cosmetic kit from her purse and steps into the line that angles to the washroom.

I once knew a man who developed a nervous disorder that prevented him from relieving himself while in a moving vehicle—not, as you might imagine, to the benefit of his health and well-being. He disgorged one day the last of what he'd swallowed into a white, wax-lined sick bag and refused to eat again. He soon died of massive internal bleeding as his body slowly cannibalized itself. The sweat of a malnourished man smells of effluvium and burning carbon. He was my friend, but most were glad to see him go.

As I return from the washroom and take my seat, I watch the televisions awaken. From panes of mirrored green, inside which the strait of our cabin tapers to a point, each resolves into focus. I find myself viewing a film depicting a rolling heath bathed in falling snow. A man is shown walking through the drifts, his footprints trailing away behind him. He stops, addresses the camera, and walks on. The man's teeth are asymmetrical and jarring. The word *Civilization* appears on the screen, somber above the blowing white snow.

Despite my complaints, were it not for television, I would know nothing of the worlds of fantasy and speculation, of astronomy and of geography. I would know nothing of mulch or antelope, sunspots or Ferris wheels; of aboriginal land claims, internecine warfare, amphibian life cycles; of rain or snow or shooting stars. I would know nothing of precipitation—of headlong descents, things that fall from the sky. This notion—of tumbling things, sheets of rain, flakes of snow, dropping as a matter of will and muffling the land and steeping the ocean—is a lovely one, but incomprehensible to all but an adept few, the meteorologists, who spend their lives engaged in highly abstruse and deeply philosophic debates, self-contained and mysterious, like nested sets of boxes, about the whys and wherefores of falling things.

Sometimes I close my eyes and envision our cabin coated in a layer of descending snow. It sits white and heavy atop seats and blankets and the queue to the washroom. It billows from ashtrays and seat pockets, whiffs in heaps against the curtains, rises from the floor and overspreads the aisles. It settles on my tongue. It melts flake by flake beneath the overhead lights and blows itself hollow beneath whistling air spouts. It covers me, envelops me, and leaves me cocooned—a tight, breathing body in a meniscus of white.

* * *

I sometimes—often—dream that I am standing in a field. Beneath my feet, and to all sides, runs an uninterrupted plane. I turn a circle, scanning the rim of the horizon. There is nothing: no trees, no hills, no knobs of land; no curtains, no people, no walls. Above me, I see two narrow rows of blinking lights. They end at the crown of my head and spire from there past a bank of clouds, aisling into the sky. Between the glint of the furthest lights, a point appears, dark against the clouds. The point grows larger, falling straight for me, and I recognize it. My mother. I awaken.

We share certain of our dreams in common: (1) *the dream of walking* (our feet strike something solid, unmoving—or, since nothing real is idle, balanced in its motion, moving first about itself and then about the sun—the earth below us, and the petals of our lungs quaver as we breathe, and the heaviness of release suffuses our bodies); (2) *the dream of rising* (we step from the portal of the plane or from the cusp of some derelict tower, a zigzaggery of corroded nails and plankwork, and we ascend—awakening, always, before we kite into the stars); (3) *the dream of chasing* (we follow something best left uncaught—a thug, a monster, a wanton, spectral hope—and find ourselves unable to stop); and (4) *the dream of appearing naked in public* (either that or in our underwear).

The dreams we share are of our fears and desires, what we feel, what we know. Myself, I know nothing—only this: from moment to moment the slow drift of emotion. I suspect, though I do not know, that the things I feel are like a clustering of bubbles, empty but for what I send into them, and that as I stray through the weeks and the years, the breath of me will change—that pain in time will become pleasure, and what I now call joy will one day weigh like strange regret upon my heart.

* * *

A bullet comes from a discharged gun, rending the air as it approaches your temple. You stand in the line of fire, twiddling your thumbs, cooling your jets. You watch with lazy eyes. The bullet is in motion. To reach you, it must first cross half the distance, the distance between gun and temple, muzzle and target. Having reached the midpoint of its journey, the bullet must cross half the distance that remains. Then half again. And again. The bullet draws closer, slowing as it approaches. Soon it is only a lash's remove from your skin. It has long since ceased to spin, and you watch it hovering there. It reposes on a cushion of air, silver scalloped ejection scars scored along its length. The bullet is halving incalculably small distances—one, then another, then another—and it moves nearer your temple with every passing snip of time. It will never reach you.

Your mother steps through the portal of a plane in flight. You watch until she drops from sight, and then you watch the clouds throwing off spumes of vapor. Somewhere down there, your mother is nearing ground. But she hasn't hit—not yet.

Motion within space or time is a mathematical impossibility, for it demands an advance across distance, which is infinitely divisible and must be traveled one division at a time: there is always a smaller division, always more distance. To die is to pass from one point, life, to another point, death, through the distance which is dying. Motion such as this is an impossibility—and while the happening of the impossible can hold true within life, it cannot hold true within dying, a process of ceasing impossibilities. Death, then, that target toward which the bullet of life is racing, is impossible—if only for the dying. A falling body is a logical proposition, and thus cannot reach ground.

The last flicker of consciousness is an object turning in upon itself, a gravitational collapse, exploring its every complexity and possibility within the smallest of forevers. Most often, I imagine, the last thought of the dying is a matter of deployed belief—though the possibilities of exception abound: a man run through by a knife blade, for instance, might die and think forever of the pain; violence, in such circumstances, becomes all the more unacceptable. Still, a dying believer might think of Heaven or Eternal Return or Submergence into the Universal Whole; a dying atheist of Nothing; a disciple of karmic transmigration either Once More or Uh-Oh, depending on the virtue of his life (and he may, between moments, lead a run of tiered and reincarnate lives, each an afterclap of the one before, all an echo of the first). Conjecture becomes more complicated in consideration of the brief glimmers of thought that pass through us when we least expect them. Falling Snow, we may think, or With My Lover, or I Am Light.

It is difficult to overestimate the potential in infinity, the depth of any single thought. We die into our vision of forever. Falling, never landing, we believe our eternity into existence.

* * *

Reports persist of curious objects, erratic and puzzling of aim, glimpsed within the sky. Witnesses speak of metallic glints seen rising from rushes of distant cloud or poised like a daylight star against the blue (sometimes, as they startle away, trailing threads of vapor in their wake). At night, winking red lights have been sighted gliding across the face of the moon and passing like wise, cold comets between the stars. Some claim that these two phenomena are one—that red is white, white is red, the same color at a sun's remove. Others swear they have seen white tinsel points of light dim and darken and wink to red as the night catches the day. Witnesses, however, remain few, and details remain sketchy.

Our archaeologists, excavating a mound of spent luggage in a disused closet, have recently discovered a brittle scrolled manuscript—gone yellow with age, black in places—that seems to record an account of such a sighting. This confirms the evidence of ancient pictographs uncovered behind the hull at the rear of our vessel. Both indicate that our ancestors believed such remote and glimmering lights to be the manifesting spirits of departed friends and relatives, portents of keen significance for those who chanced to see them. Our forebears held that a ghost might become visible by wrapping itself in swathes of surrounding air, and that, wherever spirit met sky, the dead might appear. Our scientists proclaim this an unlikely possibility.

The lights in the sky, some believe, are autonomous organisms—free-floating creatures of obscure intelligence dating from an age when life on this world was a form of behavior, the functional state of heat and light. Those who believe this refer to the lights as *critters,* deeming them harmless, if not benevolent. Others hold that the lights are frozen pools of cloud, shimmering white by day and flaring red in the darkness with retained sunlight, still others that they are crafts much like our own, peopled by a race of proud and abstracted people, a community of travelers, shy, bewildered, and self-contained. Some insist that the lights are visitors, aloof and unworldly, come from elsewhere to observe us.

So that we might come to identify them—these lights in the sky—and in order to determine the give and density of cloud cover, the material composition of wind and blue weather, the potential of the outside world for supporting human life, we have initiated a program of sky exploration. Our scientists and engineers, working in tandem, are perfecting the technology that will allow us to send a man into the sky and safely retrieve him. The latter of these two propositions, that of safe return, is of no small concern. Last year, we ejected the first of our stratonauts—a man girded by belt and hook to a hundred-yard line of elasticized rope—from the plane's front portal. Plunging the length of his tether, he bounced up and back and was snuffed into the outer port turbofan engine. Not, you may think, an auspicious debut to our fledgling sky program. I saw him emerge from the other side in a spray of bone and viscera. The engine sputtered and stalled, and it hasn't worked properly since. Our scientists and engineers decided to rethink their methods.

Our stratonauts now undergo a rigorous training regimen. They sleep in the overhead compartments, eat their meals (high-fiber cereals, peanut flour, and lots of potatoes) while spinning in brisk circles, and spend hours each day trying to squeeze themselves into the crisper of our onboard refrigeration unit—all of which, our scientists insist, will prepare them for the hardships of sky exploration. Journalists report that our sky program will recommence in a few short weeks. Hopes run high.

Talk has circulated of efforts to initiate a ground exploration program as well. Our experts, though, have been unable to formulate a viable down-to-earth strategy. Recently, they invited the general public to submit their ideas for consideration. To date, however, only one suggestion has come to light—this a proposal to outfit terranauts with parachute-cum-trampoline suits—and the prospects do not look encouraging.

The protesters onboard deem the sky program a needless expenditure of manpower and resources. Yesterday they staged a demonstration. Marching heavily through the aisles, hoisting placards and chanting unpleasantries, they were soon confronted by the stewardesses, and they dispersed to their chairs, buckled their seat belts, and decided to hold a sit-in. Our energies, they insist, could be better employed coping with present troubles. We needn't go searching for more. The underclasses are hungry, they say, and shouldn't remain so for the sake of our restlessness, our fidgeting curiosity. And, they point out, there are regions of our own vessel we have yet to fully explore: the stewardesses' lounge, for instance, the rear luggage compartment, and the room behind the metal door anterior to first class—dustproof, lightproof, and always securely locked.

* * *

It's early morning. A bend of sunlight has commenced its slow rise, a sliver of red at the line of the horizon. I am among the first of us to have woken. A child slips out of her seat and onto the floor, landing limply, like a dropped shoelace, with a whish and muted pat. She opens her eyes and, without twisting her neck, looks numbly to both sides. Yawning, she drifts back into sleep. The days and nights are of uneven duration here, depending upon our direction of flight, but still, in the end, we find comfort in habit, sleeping when it's dark and rising when it's light.

I can see the face (its features become placid, deep-settled with sleep) of the woman who lives in front of me. She's there, beautiful, through the fluting between the seats. I've promised myself that I'll talk to her today. In five months' time she may have had a child. I will be the father, she the mother. Every day she passes me in the aisle, and I think I've noticed her gaining weight. When I talk to her, I won't say that. It will be: you're my favorite person here, and I'm sorry I don't know how to speak with you, where to start or who you are, but in truth, you terrify me. I'll have to see where it goes from there.

A child. It's an unsettling and exhilarating hope, a promise threading through the blood and breath of my ancestry. Quite ridiculous that it might have come about in this way, a disarray of limbs and fluids beneath a woolen blanket. My child is approaching this world by means of dead reckoning, stumbling geotactically through mute, ancient hallways, through chains of chemistry and sequences of pure mathematics. To think, my baby boy or girl, that what you become depends on how I live. To think how thick with elsewhere you'll arrive.

I miss you, mother.

Dawn is rising, and the world is breaking open like a shell. We smell the coffee brewing like oil, like a fiesta, in the first-class cabin. We stir from sleep. The green panes of the televisions break into light, their screens lamping over the seats as our dreams go glimmering away. Beneath me, the tips of drifting clouds open brilliantly. They look, the clouds, like some soaring firmament of architecture—solid and compact, unyielding. If I jumped from here, they would break my fall. I would brush myself off and salute this plane as it roared away. I would drink deep breaths and drift through space. I would walk the cloud footpaths, swing wide the gates, and climb the cloud stairs to my bed in the castle.

Sometimes I find myself thinking that I'm going somewhere, that all of this motion is indeed a motion toward, that into the trail we leave behind us, wrapping this world like a net, will fall our destination. Sometimes I find myself thinking that I'm going somewhere, until I realize that I'm already there.

The Light through the Window

There was once a window cleaner who lived on the seventy-first floor of a great glass building. Each morning he donned his jumpsuit, his boots, and his sky-colored cap, then climbed from his bedroom window onto a wooden platform with taut wire rigging. He turned the heavy steel winches that, side by side, reminded him of the infinity symbol—the one that lowered and raised him, the other that trolleyed him along each floor—and all day long he washed the windows of his building. He sprayed them with his misting hose as the sun rose through the morning and sank through the afternoon. He planed them dry with a rubber-edged blade as the curtains behind them slid open and shut. This was in the days when motorcars flowed through the city like a river of silver mercury, and he often listened to the gust of traffic as he rubbed at gummy spots with a cotton rag. The high wind sent drops of water rolling up the glass. His shadow slanted away beneath him. If he worked diligently, he could complete three and a half floors by late afternoon, and when the windows went orange with the setting sun, he would remove his cap and hoist himself home. Once he left his window open to a spring breeze in order to air his apartment, and when he returned that night to his bed, he found a robin trapped beside him in the sheets. It thrashed and struggled there like a heart, and when he freed it, it flew into a wall. He carried it to the wastebasket on the end of a dustpan. Afterward he always sealed the window tight behind him.

Sometimes at night, unable to sleep, the window cleaner would sit at the edge of his platform and try to count the lights of the city: he watched them sailing red and white through the streets, twinkling from lampposts and porches, hanging in the blackness of tall buildings—so many lights, and within each one a life. The window cleaner wondered how it would feel to be in the thick of them, to be some other person, in a restaurant drinking with friends or in a bed with his arm around his lover. The thought that he had never married or fathered children often filled him with a quiet sadness, and on Sunday afternoons, with little else to do, he imagined himself in one of the small, glistening motorcars on the street, driving across the river with his family. They would go to a carnival, perhaps, or a shopping mall, and the boys would fight with each other in the back seat, and he would feed them hot dogs and french fries until they were groggy and quiet.

Certainly, though, the window cleaner loved his work. He wasn't the first of his family to tend these windows: he had learned the trade from his father and grandfather—both of them window cleaners, both of them now gone. As a small boy he had ridden along as they scrubbed side by side, watching the pop-tabs he'd collected in his pockets spin to the ground when he snapped them off the platform. In the chill of the evening he would ascend with the men to the seventy-first floor—once the apex of the building, though it had since been overtopped by floors seventy-two through two hundred eight—where his mother would be waiting to lift him inside. When he came of age, it was the three of them on that platform, though soon enough it was two, and then it was only him. To this day, when his reflection split in the panes of double windows, he sometimes saw their figures standing dimly beside him.

What he learned from the men of his family was this: that a blue sky on a new day is a better thing than most; that there is fineness and value in a surface you can't see; and that with just a slant of light and a film of water, he could write himself into the rooms behind the glass.

When he felt the clean white heat of the sun against his shoulders, all he had to do was squeeze the grip of his misting hose, spray a haze of fine moisture on the window, and spell his message in it with a finger. Then, stepping aside to remove his shadow, he could read what he had written. The sunlight would catch in the dampness, turning silver, but it would pour sharply through the marks he'd left. It would burst onto the walls or carpets, posting his words there until he cleared them away with his rubber-edged blade. Such light could transform glass into a mirror, but the window cleaner stood so close to the building that he had little difficulty seeing into it, and in the slow hours of bright days, he found this a happy diversion. When he saw someone he recognized, he often wrote his hello. When faced with a messy sitting room (its plants wilting, chairs toppled, picture frames askew) he might write *Junkyard* or *Pigsty* or *Just Not Clean*—and, looking inside, find the words floating there like a label. Though the people in these rooms sometimes noticed him, frequently they did not. Once, in an access of sympathy, he wrote *Bless You* on the office window of a businessman, and when the sun projected it onto his desk, the man sneezed seven times in sequence without ever looking up.

One balmy spring day the window cleaner was trolleying himself across the west side of the forty-second floor, straying through his memories as he turned the winch. He had just eaten his lunch and was recalling the time his father froze a gold ring with a cap of diamonds into an ice cube for his tenth wedding anniversary. He himself was only a boy then, and so he had been asleep when his parents returned from the terrace restaurant, but his mother told him the next morning that she'd almost swallowed the ring before she saw the glint.

Stopping at the corner of the building, the window cleaner took a drink of water from his thermos. His platform swayed in a gust of wind. Far below him, a pair of children raced along the berm kicking at dandelions. When he turned to the window, he saw a woman rolling across her office in a desk chair. She was gazing at the ceiling, hands joined behind her neck as she walked herself across the carpet, and she was singing something. She seemed strangely familiar. Sometimes, when you yawn or shout, you will hear a noise like the clicking of a beetle, and suddenly the world will sound twice as rich as before. The window cleaner felt something similar happen inside him—a budding in his lungs: the world he was breathing seemed suddenly twice as wide. He activated his misting hose, and in its drizzle the sunlight fractured into seven colors. Then, on the window, he wrote the words *Will,* and *You,* but he didn't know how to continue. He stood there for a moment. He peeked past the haze and saw the woman smiling from her roller-chair, but he could not tell if she saw him.

When his hand began to twitch, he brought it to his side. When he stepped from the light, his shadow stepped with him. He lay awake for hours that night, listening to the barking of far dogs.

The light from past moments is not lost forever: every star, every city, every family and person sends each instant of its light into the measure of surrounding space—and though such rays disperse in all directions, there are forces that can draw them back together. Thus it was that the window cleaner was not wholly surprised when the next morning, in the dark of a coming storm, he saw from his platform a vision that was many years past. Sponging the dirt from his rubber-edged blade, he detected the rush of an approaching platform. As it neared, he recognized it as his own. His grandfather was handling the winches, his silver wristwatch glinting as he pumped. His father stood pointing into the sky (at a cloud? a jet? a thunderstorm?), and his mother touched her hand to the small of his back: she was carrying a child—she was carrying *him*—and her belly was as round as a sail. The window cleaner followed behind them as they skirted the corner of the building. Though he could not hear them speaking, he could see them in all their sharpness and color—the snap of youth in his grandfather's eyes, his mother's red-brown hair streaming in the wind. When they halted at the living room window, he drifted in above them and lay on the deck of the platform, peering over its edge. His father folded a hand around his mother's stomach, then held her as she clambered inside. They kissed before she shut the window, kissed once more through the glass, and then wavered like shadows in a guttering flame. When they vanished, the window cleaner lay staring at the sudden space beneath him. The white headlamps of motorcars shone against the dark street, and columns of windows shimmered in the air. It was raining. He descended a floor and, tingling wet, stepped into the stillness of his apartment. The living room window grew steamy with his breath as he searched for the splash-mark of his parents' lips.

The storm lasted for several days, and then one afternoon a cool salt wind blew in from the ocean, sweeping it into the distance. The lines of the building grew sharp beneath the spring sky, and the window cleaner felt in the cycling of his blood the tug of something like a promise. He pulled himself to the west side of the forty-second floor and began misting the corner window, smoothing it clean, and misting it again. He had a question for the woman in the roller-chair, and he stood silently rehearsing it until her door wheeled open in a flash of yellow light. She entered the room with a hurried stride, stooping to place a leather satchel against the baseboard. When he rapped on the window, she started. He waved to her in greeting, and politely, but with an air of consternation, she waved back. As she lifted her jacket onto a wall peg, he knocked once more. She turned and mouthed a phrase that he couldn't decipher, then took a step forward, arms akimbo. He beckoned her closer, writing *Will* as she approached and *You* as she looked at him with hard gray eyes. Then she frowned and, drawing the curtains closed, vanished.

The window cleaner felt a dwindling sensation in his chest and stomach.

Though he tapped a few times at her window, the woman did not reappear.

The glass of the city soon went orange with the evening sunlight. He listened to the horn blasts of passing traffic, watched a flight of martins darting from an alley, and was taken by a blaze of sudden energy. It was a hard flash of sickness and embarrassment and anger.

He coiled his misting hose and cranked the winches of his platform, propelling it from the corner of the forty-second floor. Its rigging whistled and its planking creaked as he sailed from face to face of the building. Its side rail shook like a dowsing rod as he tumbled and dipped and ascended. He orbited the cornice of floor two hundred eight, and he buzzed a peanut peddler on the sidewalk. The sun flashed blue as it sank behind a distant bridge. A cotton rag slipped from the deck of his platform, fluttering away like a lazy white moth.

All this time, as he watched the darkening of the world, the window cleaner thought about the farawayness of other lives, about the fraying wire that bound him to his wishes, about the kindnesses of people who were now no more than ghosts. But as the stars began to brighten overhead—singly or in little clusters, and never at regular intervals—he ceased to think about these things. His hands slowed at the winches, and his body filled with rest, and he thought instead about the dandelion feathers that even the gentlest breeze could carry to the fiftieth floor, the sunlight that turned his shadow around him each day like a clock hand, the way the entire visible world can become caught in the glass of a polished window. He thought about his heart that flickered like a candleflame and his lungs that contracted like a bellows.

As he glided to a stop beside his bedroom window, the window cleaner saw two figures standing at his dressing chest. He recognized the first as his grandfather and the other, a small boy straining toward the light switch, as himself.

The boy pecked at the wall with his hand, and for a moment everything went dark. Then the window cleaner saw the loose shapes of their bodies concentrating as if from a white fog as they approached. They walked quietly beside each other, the man's palm on the boy's shoulder, and they did not seem to notice him. When they reached the window they stopped before him. He watched his grandfather lift a misting bottle from his pocket, spraying until a haze of water appeared on the glass, all the while gesturing in instruction to his grandson. Then, satisfied, he stepped to the side. With a shrug of hesitation, the small boy scribbled something in the moisture, and he turned to his grandfather, who nodded. The old man unhooked a flashlight from his belt loop and held it toward the window. When the light streamed like a beacon through the strokes in the mist, the window cleaner watched his own young eyes fill with recognition behind the glass, his own hand float slowly to his lips, his grandfather smile and ruffle his hair. And in the brisk night wind, as he stood on the platform heavy with sleep, he traced the light, and bowed his head, and saw written across his own drumming chest his name.

The House at the End of the World

When I was four years old, and living with my father, I would wait in the well of an oak tree each morning for him to come home, listening for the sound of his boots on the forest floor. The oak tree was an old black giant that stood by our front door. It grew acorns the size of my fist, and its trunk was mottled with a dry gray moss. Every morning when the sun climbed onto my window sill, I would run to the tree and crawl inside. The hollow I liked to sit in was spacious and deep, and I was such a small girl that I fit there easily. I would wait and listen, dreaming up little fantasies to pass the time, and then the leaves would crack, and the twigs would snap, and I'd know that my father was coming home.

Our ceremony was this: he would place the food he had caught on a wooden platform by the front door—on some days a fish or a bird, on others a beaver or rabbit. He would knock the mud from his boots, then step over to the oak tree and slap it playfully with his palm—a hard, living sound. "Oak tree," he would sigh. "You're my only friend in all the world. I had a daughter once, a girl who loved me, but she's gone now and I don't know where to find her." I would listen quietly, and when my father had finished delivering his lines, I would spring from beneath him shouting, "Here I am, here I am." He would sweep me into the air and blanket me with kisses. "Ah, Holly," he would say. Ah, father.

This was during the collapse of civilization, and I believed we were the only people in the world. My father had made certain preparations for these times: in a storeroom off our kitchen were cases of nails and soap and matches. On a shelf above the door stood a set of oil lamps, their globes polished to a liquid shine, and beside them was a box of spare wicks and several containers of lamp oil. A bolt of cotton cloth was leaning rigidly against the corner wall. A tool chest was tucked behind a stack of towels. We had a caulking gun and a sewing treadle and a crank flashlight with an electric socket in the butt. (We had a crank radio, as well, on a table in my father's bedroom, but it was busted and would produce no sound, not even the fuzz of static.) And then there were the canned goods, large metal cylinders that lined the walls of our pantry, stacked three or four cans deep in columns that were staggered in height. These columns looked like steel pillars, or organ pipes, and when I walked into the pantry with a lamp or a candle I would see thousands of tiny flames flickering about me. There was powdered milk and coffee, rice and wheat and oats and flour, sugar and corn meal, beans and granola. There were carrots and eggs and hard little nuggets of dried potato. My favorite cans were the ones along the front wall, which held chocolate pudding, orange marmalade, and applesauce, and whenever we opened one, I would stand at my father's side and breathe in that first wonderful smell which came through the puncture.

Our house itself was built beside a stream of swift, clear water in the eye of the forest. Trees pressed against the back wall and then cleared away in the front yard, rising up again on the other side of a meadow. I sometimes thought of the forest as a river and of our house as one of those shoulders of stone that interrupts the current—my father and I were like the fish you find living in the shadows. Two trails stretched from our yard into the trees, one to a blackberry thicket and one to a cluster of birches where we gathered kindling. We had a small garden where we grew potatoes and carrots and pale, misshapen zucchini. In the meadow were mushrooms and clover and, in the spring, small purple flowers that smelled of mustard when you crushed them between your fingers. The grass was not high—we must have walked across it a hundred times a day—and deer occasionally stopped there to wrap themselves in the sunlight; if I clapped my hands, they would bound back into the trees through the loose, cottony brush. I was content in our house. In my bed at night I felt safe and warm. The world had ended. The stream splashed before me, and the forest stirred behind me. My father worked quietly in the next room.

My father was a natural mender of things. At night, for instance, he would tinker with little objects around the house, even the things that were irreparably broken. Every few days he would work for an hour or so on the small electric generator we owned. The generator had lost some basic internal mechanism, and though it looked easy to fix, in all the time I lived with him he was never successful. A few yards into the woods was a place where the stream banks narrowed and the water began to race, and he had placed a dam there and fitted it with a turbine. With this turbine and the generator, he had hoped to produce enough electricity to light the house, but instead he made a simple wheel for me to play with.

One summer afternoon, a few months after my fourth birthday, I found a turtle wedged beneath the turbine. I had taken a pair of pliers from my father's tool chest, setting off into the woods to play fix-the-dam, and when I got there the turtle was submerged in the water. She was trying to push herself free. The long shaft of her neck was reaching from beneath the current of the stream, and her legs were shunting back and forth in the clay. I was afraid that she would suffocate—her head would drop from exhaustion, and she would be trapped without air beneath the water—so I pulled her loose and the turbine began to spin again, throwing off drops of water. I carried the turtle inside and showed her to my father. He held her in his hands.

"Did you know that turtles are like trees?" he said. "You can tell how old they are by counting the plates on their shell."

"Really?" I asked.

"Of course. Here, I'll show you." We counted the fourteen plates on the turtle's shell, one by one. "So she's fourteen years old," my father said. He tapped on the shell, then peered in through the opening in the front, trying to spot the turtle's head. "Where's my tool chest?" he asked. I pointed. "Get me a paint marker, will you?"

I ran to the other side of the room and brought him a thick red marker. It made a rattling sound when he shook it and gave off a sharp bleachlike smell. He wrote my name in capital letters on the turtle's rearmost plate: HOLLY. "There," he said, and he blew gently on the paint to dry it. "Now if we see her again, we'll know she's ours." He capped the marker and held the turtle at arm's length, examining his writing in a shaft of sunlight. "That's what your name means," he said. "Did I ever tell you that? 'Turtle.'"

The lessons my father taught me rarely left me feeling any wiser. They only deepened my awareness of everything I would never know.

* * *

One day that fall I was walking alongside the stream, following a boat I had made from a strip of birch bark and some epoxy glue. It hit an eddy, and I tapped it loose with a stick, and then my father came up behind me and rested his hand on my shoulder. "The *Marie Celeste,*" he said solemnly. "The boat without captain or crew."

"I made it in the kitchen," I said. "I didn't glue my fingers together." This is what he always asked me when I told him that I'd been building something: Did you glue your fingers together? If I answered yes, he would wrap his hands around them and pretend that he couldn't pull them apart.

He fished the boat from the water and set it on the shore. "Let me tell you about the *Marie Celeste.*"

I propped myself against the high dirt bank of the stream, listening.

"It was a ghost ship. The story goes that sailors would see it traveling toward them in the fog. Its masts were always raised, its walls always straight, and they would signal for it to change course so that it wouldn't sail into them. When it drew near, though, they would find it deserted—no men on deck, no lights inside, nothing. Somebody boarded it once and found clothes hanging on the wash lines. Beds were rumpled in the shapes of bodies, dinner plates were black with grease. The captain's log was still open on his desk. Whatever had happened there had happened fast. Nobody was ever able to bring the *Marie Celeste* into shore, and every now and then you would hear another report of it. It seemed to sail itself, people said. The ocean is a big place, so you never know. Maybe it's still out there."

I had never seen the ocean and I tried to imagine it. All I could envision was our field on the days when it flooded, the surface of the water dimpled by blades of grass.

My father lifted me onto the bank of the stream, standing me on my feet.

"Take a walk with me," he said.

Not far from our house, less than half an hour's travel, was a cave which the heat of the sun never seemed to penetrate. We had taken shelter there once during a violent summer rain, and even then the air was as cold and still as the frozen air of winter. I could see my breath in the cave, and I enjoyed watching the shapes it made: mushroom shapes, and apple shapes, and finger shapes. The water, which stood in pools at the entrance, always wore a thick shell of ice, and if we chipped at this ice and wrapped the larger pieces in rags, we could carry them home before they melted.

As we hiked through the forest, I tried to match my step to my father's, but his pace was much quicker than mine, his stride much longer. He could step over patches of mud that I had to leap. He could climb onto logs without using his hands. "Slow down," I kept calling, and he would turn and wait for me, fanning himself with his T-shirt.

After a while, I began to feel winded, and I asked him a question, knowing from experience that as he spoke he would slow down in thought. "Did *you* ever see the *Marie Celeste*?" I said.

"No," he said. "No, I've never even been on a boat, actually." He began to slow down. "But I did read about it. And I heard stories. People used to tell stories about all sorts of strange things." A switch of thorns was bending into the path, and he held it out of the way for me as I walked past. "Ghosts and fairies. Lake monsters and UFOs. You have to wonder what's become of all that now that we're gone. The ghosts, for instance: let's say they were real. Were they haunting *us,* then, or were they haunting the places where we found them? And if they were haunting *us,* did they disappear when we did, or are they still floating around out there inside all those empty houses? Are they anything without us? What did we mean to them?"

Nearby, a squirrel sat on a yellow log taking apart a pine cone. My father ducked beneath a vine, and I followed him.

"If I vanished today, Holly, what would you do?" he said. His voice was gentle. I took his sleeve. "You would miss me at first, but how long would it be before I came to seem like a dream to you? How long before you could live happily without even a thought of me? I hope I've been able to give you the things you need."

I had never asked myself these questions before, but I knew that if my father were to leave me, or to give up his life somewhere in the forest, I would be utterly lost and alone. The animals were stronger than me, larger and faster and quieter on their feet, and the house grew cold and dark at night, and I would not know what to do. Even the lanterns, on their shelves in the storeroom, were too high for me to reach without my father. I began to cry.

"Oh, hey," he said, bending over to console me. "Hey, hey, hey." He kissed my cheek, and my forehead, and rubbed a tear away with his thumb. "I'm not going anywhere, baby. You don't have to worry. I didn't mean to upset you."

I felt the weight of his arm on my shoulder, and when I swallowed a breath, I could smell the faint palm scent of the soap that he used and the strong spice of his sweat, a smell that still today I associate with my father. "Are you going to be okay?" he asked. I nodded. And then, looking up, I realized we were at the cave.

I sat inside on a ridge of stone as my father chipped at a frozen puddle. He took a hammer from his pocket, then knocked at the ice with the claw of the hammer until it came apart with a crack. When it was time to go, he bundled a few of the larger chunks in a scarf and we stepped outside. The sudden change in temperature made me feel dizzy. One of my legs buckled, and my head seemed to fill with pieces of shimmering light, like the reflection of the sun from broken water. I didn't think I could walk back to the house.

"Carry me," I said to my father.

"Make you a deal," he said. "I'll carry you, if you carry the ice."

He hoisted me onto his back, and I tucked the ice against my side. I could feel the muscles of my stomach tightening against the cold.

The back of my father's neck was a reddish brown color, and the skin there was folded into a slight X. I watched this X open and contract, and felt my body adjusting to the rhythm of his stride, as he walked us home across the forest.

It was not long after that that my father broke his arm, and I learned to bait the traps, and draw the water, and operate the machinery of our world.

I was sitting in the living room cutting dolls from a brown paper sack when the front door swung open, banging heavily into the wall. My father stumbled toward me. He did not shut the door behind him, and a dry maple leaf came blowing in across the floor, skittering on its legs like a spider. "I need you to do something for me, Holly," he said. He spoke calmly but tears were rolling down his face. His breathing was ragged. "Do you know the way to the cave? Can you get there by yourself?"

"Are you okay?" I asked.

"Daddy hurt himself." I looked at his arm: beneath the elbow it was twisted and swollen, and the hair there, painted with blood, was flattened to his skin. He said, "I need you to get me some ice. Can you do that? Can you hurry?"

I could. I ran to the cave, watching the trunks of great trees slide past me like creatures in a dream, the gaps in the branches showing flashes of white sky. I was surprised by how little my body grew tired. I did not think to bring a hammer, so I slammed at the ice with a hoof-shaped stone, and I did not think to bring a rag, so I wrapped the chunks in my shirt to carry them home.

My father had treated his wound with alcohol and a sterile cotton pad, securing his arm in a temporary sling. When I arrived home with the ice, he loosened the bandages.

"All right," he said. "Now I need you to do something else for me. I need you to take my arm"—he touched the thick barrow of muscle just beneath his shoulder—"and hold it tight. Don't let go, okay?"

I did as he said, clenching his arm to my chest.

"Are you ready?" he asked.

Before I could say yes, he grabbed hold of his arm and, pulling hard, hitched it into place. The bone made a grating sound and then it gave a sudden pop. My father screamed, lurching in his chair, and I fell backward and lost my grip.

"God-*damn* it!" he shouted.

"I'm sorry, I'm sorry," I said. I thought that by letting go I had torn something loose inside him: it was the scream he had made, and the tightening of his face. "I tried to hold on."

His eyes were squeezed shut and he sighed—a weary, lingering breath. "Okay," he said to himself, breathing deeply. "Okay. I'll be all right. Everything's going to be all right." He placed the ice I had brought him around the break, and a few minutes later he removed it and strapped his arm into a splint.

That afternoon he took to his bed.

It was more than a week before he left the house, and more than a month before he was able to venture back into the forest. During that time I took on the work of our family, caring for him as best I could.

I woke when the sky was still violet. The air was always cold at that hour, and the first whistles of the birds could almost be mistaken for a part of the silence. I checked the traps on the far side of the stream, rebaiting the ones that had been touched off during the night. I caught small iridescent fish that turned gray when they reached the air. I gathered wood and picked mushrooms and carried water to the house in a green plastic bucket. I learned how to sift through coals for glowing orange embers and how to blow sparks from them to start a fire. I learned how to gut and cook the fish that I caught. I learned how to open cans with a can opener, biting securely into the lid and then twisting the handle in a circle. I learned how to sweep floors and change bandages and oil the hinges of our weathered front door. So many things are mysteries until you have experienced them. I felt as though I was learning to be my father.

Every day, when I had finished my early morning chores, I would prepare a breakfast of boiled oats for him and knock on his bedroom door. He would be waiting for me there, just as I had waited for him in the mossy hollow of the oak tree. I was filled—constantly filled—with a sense of surprise at my own skill, my own capability, and each morning I took more of my father's heart into my care. "How's your arm?" I would ask.

"Stiff," he would say. "Stiff, but getting better." His hair was always crisp from sleep, his room always musty. I would watch as he added honey and milk to his oatmeal. "Did we catch anything in the traps?" he would ask.

"No," I would answer. "The animals just eat the bait and wander off into the woods."

He would say, "Those traps aren't worth mud."

I would agree with him: "They're pretty useless, all right."

There we were, the two of us talking together like grown men, and this meant all the world to me.

Afterward I would help him get dressed—maneuvering his broken arm through his shirt sleeve, lacing and knotting his boots for him. Then we would play cards together or wash clothes together or sit together and listen to the flow of the stream, which was running shallow that season. He might read me a story as I chopped and mixed the ingredients for dinner. He might steady the ladder as I climbed into the storeroom to get some lamp oil. Sometimes he would worry that his arm wasn't setting properly. "Should it still be hurting?" he would ask. "I'm not in any pain right now, but the break stabs at me whenever I try to move it. I just wish I could get rid of this stupid splint. You shouldn't have to work so hard, Holly," he would say. "I want to be able to take care of you. We need each other."

One day as I was standing in the woods, peeling a strip of birch bark into threads of tinder, a bear came lumbering through the brush and stopped not ten yards away from me. It was a small black bear, the fur around its face specked with some kind of snowlike grain, and it gave off a wet, slightly stale smell. Bears are perhaps the most human of all the forest creatures, and they can seem strangely impassive at times. This one simply looked me in the eye for a moment, turned on its legs, and swung away.

When I got home, I told my father what had happened. His eyes creased with alarm. "Are you sure you don't want me to teach you to use the gun?"

"I'm sure," I said. I had fired a gun once—or rather, I had held the carriage of a gun against my shoulder as my father pulled the trigger. I found the noise it made frightening, and liked neither the smell that rose from the barrel nor the way it kicked back against me when it fired, which made it seem alive. As I answered my father, my life seemed completely within my control, a good feeling. I was strong and smart and proud. I was capable of making my own decisions. I was only five years old—almost five years old—but I was growing into my adulthood.

Still, at night, as the birds slowly stopped their singing and the insects slowly began their own, I would become a child again. My father and I would watch the stars come up one by one through the crowns of the trees, and after a while we would head inside. I was always sleepy from all the work I had done, and he would usually have to squeeze my hand to keep me from drifting away. After I had helped him out of his T-shirt, he would tuck me into bed and sing me a lullaby, and then, gradually, I would fall asleep:

All the world is gone away,
All the light and all the gray
Of buildings, houses, streets, and schools,

All the wishes, all the rules,
Of everybody, everywhere,
Oh, all their dreams and all their cares.
Our loved ones and our dearest friends
Are waiting at the journey's end.
The moon is high, the night is deep.
Hush now, baby, go to sleep.

* * *

Though his arm never did heal perfectly—he experienced a dull pain in damp weather, and there was a glossy line just below the elbow where the hair would not grow—my father was soon able to untie his bandages and remove the splint. He seemed to fill with his old remembered energy. He could walk long miles into the forest, he could hunt and he could fish, and he could carry me without difficulty. We resumed the pattern of our lives.

The stream in our front yard was running thinner than it ever had before. It was our only reliable source of water, and now it was fogged with silt—that is, where there was any current at all. There were places where it ran so shallow that the water seemed to be simply filtering up from the earth. Winter was nearing its end, and the last few months had seen pale white skies and little rain, but this in itself was not unusual and the stream had never flowed so weakly before. It was as if the land which had for so long given us shelter was finally reconsidering its bounty. I half expected to see the blackberry bushes reabsorbing their fruit, the grass shrinking back into the mud, the trees and saplings taking in their branches like umbrellas.

After my father roused me from my place in the oak tree one day, he decided to head into the forest to investigate. He thought that there might be a plug of wood damming the stream somewhere, or that the bank might have collapsed, diverting the water into an adjacent streambed. He told me that he was going to walk a few miles upstream and that he would be back by late afternoon.

I passed the time whittling a small chunk of hickory into a spinning top: the flesh of the wood was tough, the fibers sinewy, and try as I might I was unable to perfect the balance. My father returned home as the sun was sinking into the trees and casting a quiet red light on the grass and the clover. He sat down beside me at the saddle of the front door and took off his shoes, flexing the muscles of his feet.

"Well?" I asked.

"Not a thing," he said. He had hiked along the ledge of the stream for more than five hours, crossing to the other side when he hit a thicket or a patch of thorns, sometimes walking in the streambed itself. In all that time, he said, he had never seen the current grow wider than his wrist. "The water's not disappearing along the way, it's simply not there."

"You didn't see anything at all?"

"Nothing," he said. "Well, nothing that might explain where the water's going. I did see Holly the Turtle. She's living beneath a stand of roots about an hour away from here." He smiled and tousled my hair. "She sends her regards."

Now and then, when I saw a turtle scuffing through the leaves, I had wondered about Holly in the idle way you wonder about those small things in your life that have disappeared. I wholly expected to see the little red signet of my name vanishing behind a log one day, or lolloping around the corner of the house. How likely is it that such a creature will circle back through the world to find you once again?

I don't know, but I have heard the same story in other shapes, and I never doubted my father.

Later that evening, he confessed his worries to me. While he could filter the dirt from the water and boil it free of any impurities, he wasn't sure what we would do if the stream ran completely dry. What if we awoke one morning to find the streambed jigsawed with cracks? It sent a nervous flutter through his stomach. "I have an idea, though," he said. "What I want to do is travel up-forest a few days and see if I can learn anything. If I go, though, Holly, I might be gone for as long as a week. Will you be okay if I'm gone that long? Do you think you can take care of yourself?"

"Couldn't I go with you?"

My father hoisted me onto his lap. "I don't think that would be a good idea. First of all, I don't know what I'll find. And then what would we do if you got hurt? How would we take care of you?" He jogged his leg, steadying me with his hand. "No, I don't want to leave you here, but it's the only way."

I was unconvinced, though, and that night, as he filled his backpack with food and blankets and his first aid kit, I decided that I would follow him into the forest the next morning. After all, I had taken care of him when he broke his arm. What would happen if *he* got hurt, far from home, with no one who loved him?

My father woke me early in the morning, while the night was still dark. His eyes reflected two tiny threads of light from the lantern in his hands, which was burning dimly. "I'm leaving now, Holly. Don't forget to check the traps when you wake up. Treat any scrapes you get with iodine. Don't walk too far from home. The wood is stacked in the pantry. The tool chest is in the living room. I've left a lamp out for you. You can open a few extra cans if you want." His eyes were wet with tears. "I guess that's it. You'll be just fine." He kissed me on the cheek. "Bye, sweetness."

I waited until I heard the front door click shut, and then I hurried outside. I was already dressed and had packed a small satchel for myself full of food and a change of clothing. As I stepped out into the predawn coolness, I was just able to spot the misty outline of my father vanishing into the trees. I knew that he would follow the course of the stream, and that I could pursue him without difficulty, but I did not want to lose sight of him. I walked as quickly as I could into the forest.

All morning I hid behind trees and boulders and nests of briar as I trailed behind him. A purple light spread across the forest floor, brightening as the sun climbed into the sky, and when I looked up, I noticed the tight yellow buds of leaves twitching on the tips of the tree branches. I tried to stay far enough behind my father so that he wouldn't hear me, walking so that when I held my thumb at arm's length it covered his body. Once, he stopped to pick the burrs from his socks: he carefully disengaged each one, flicking them out over the stream, and when he finished, he happened to glance up in my direction. My heart began to hammer in my chest, and I felt a needlelike frost dissolve though my fingers and toes. It was only by luck that he didn't discover me.

It was not until noon that I gave myself away. The stream took an ell, and my father was concealed from me by a screen of poplars. When I rounded the corner, he was standing there wiping the sweat from his brow. He started when he saw me and then his mouth lengthened into a slow smile, which he tried to stifle. He shook his head and placed his hands on his hips.

"Well," he said, "come on then."

We traveled through the forest for two days and nights. The

stream branched occasionally into separate channels, and we always followed the larger of the two.

One afternoon, I found a circle of clay-brown mushrooms in a field of grass. "It's actually a single organism," my father said. "The ring spreads underneath the soil, and the mushrooms you see are all part of that one circle. The largest living thing on earth is a fungus just like that. It spreads for miles beneath the ground, and its stalks perforate entire fields. You could build your house on top of it without even realizing it was there. The world is a big place, Holly."

At night, we would clear an area in the brush and build a low fire, walling it in with rocks. I would dig at the embers with a stick and ask my father to tell me stories. "Tell me about my mother again," I said to him one night.

"There's not much to tell," he said. "Your mother and I met when we were just kids. She was working in a grocery store, and she had the most sweet, painful smile I'd ever seen—as if every celebration she made was in the face of some greater sorrow. We talked about getting married. We moved away together. I thought we would never be separated. You were born just before the collapse, Holly. Your mother knew it was coming—we both knew—but she said that she wouldn't run away. We had to leave her behind, the two of us." He sighed. "She's gone now, just like everybody else. Her name was Megan. Best not to think about it."

Early on the morning of our third day in the forest, we climbed across a rain-eaten fence of barbed wire and emerged from the brush onto a stretch of concrete. The concrete extended for as far as I could see on the right, slicing through the trees in a gray ribbon, and on the left it disappeared over a small hill. Its surface was stained with the rust-colored prints of leaves, some of them as large as both my hands placed side to side, and I could see brown and orange and slate-blue pebbles embedded there.

As I turned to ask my father where we were, something came booming up over the hill. It glinted in the sun, and sounded its horn, and rolled by us on its many wheels. Behind it was a trailer carrying a stack of trees, stripped of their branches and lying flat on their sides. It moved as fast as anything I'd ever seen, splitting the air as it passed.

"I'll be damned," said my father.

A soft breeze came up. A dragonfly buzzed.

We stood for a long time watching the cars and trucks pass on the roadway.

When I was five years old, and living with my father, I would draw pictures of our house as an empty space in the trees: the carpet of leaves formed the floor, the branches the slope of the roof, two interlocking saplings the frame of the door. Sometimes I would draw myself inside, a small girl in a blue cotton dress, holding a broomstick or sitting in the doorway. We began to construct new dams along the gutter of the stream. The water was still flowing in a very thin trickle, and my father said that we should create what reservoirs we could while there was still time. At night I would hear him breathing in sleep from the room next door, and if I balanced my breathing to match his own, I would soon fall asleep myself. We would work together in the mornings and eat together in the evenings, and in the slowest hours of midday we would sit outside and listen to the grasses rustling in the wind. And then, when I was five years old, my mother came to take me away.

It was the beginning of spring, and while most of the trees had not yet blossomed, the magnolias were already flowering out. I was in the pantry retrieving a box of matches when I heard a loud banging at the front door. At first I thought it was my father—that he was carrying a load of wood, perhaps, and needed my help getting inside—but then his footsteps went tapping across the floor and I heard the door wheeling open on its hinges. What must he have thought as my mother's face swung into view? Did his heart beat faster, his eyes mist over? Did he know why she was there? Did it seem to him at that moment that a ghost had risen to haunt him? Or had he come to suspect (always known?) that my mother was still alive?

I don't have the answers, and it's too late to ask.

From my hiding place in the pantry I heard an unfamiliar voice. "Hello, Paul," it said. "We've come for Holly." There was a pause, during which the grain of the voice, which had been trembling, descended and took on certitude. "What have you done with her?"

My father said something then, but his own voice was faint, the words all but indistinguishable. I recognized only the occasional fragment: . . . *can't* . . . *why* . . . *I didn't* . . .

"Where's Holly?" the first voice interrupted him.

It was followed by another, a rich male baritone that carried a slight humming sound. "Best that you tell us," it said, and I imagined, because of the humming sound, that bees were rolling through it, bouncing from word to word. "We've had a hard day."

My father did not answer. The population of my world had just doubled, and its new inhabitants knew me by name: this was an astonishing thing, and though I was frightened, I wanted to see the faces of these other people—people who were speaking and breathing and moving, and who were not dead—inside my own house.

"Sir, are you going to cooperate with us?" a third voice said.

"Look at this place," the woman stabbed the words out. "First you run away with her: I come home, and you're just gone. And then where do you take her? To a shack! In the middle of the woods! I want to see my daughter, and I want to see her now."

I decided to step out from the pantry.

As I touched the living room floor, a great heaviness materialized in me. My father was standing in the middle of the room, clearly stunned. In the doorway was a woman with deep green eyes and short, honey-blond hair, flanked by two men, one in a crisp blue uniform, the other in rumpled blue jeans and a red sweater. They all looked silently at me for a moment. I looked back at them. Then the woman, my mother, came forward, bent to her knees, and folded her arms around me. She sank her head onto my shoulder and pressed a heavy kiss against the side of my neck. Her back began to shudder, and I could tell that she was going to cry.

"Oh, my baby," she whispered.

I struggled away from her and ran and stood behind my father.

The woman rose to her feet. "Holly?" she said. She took a step closer and ventured her hand. "Do you remember me, Holly?"

I shook my head no, and there was a long silence.

"I'm your mother," she said, and at that her face tied up and she gave a tiny smile.

I remembered the conversations my father and I had had about my mother—her love for him, her smile, her death in the great collapse.

And I remembered her name: "Megan." I stated it as a fact.

She questioned me with her eyes. "Yes . . . ?"

I understood then that there was something I was expected to say, something that would make sense of everything, that would piece the three of us together like a puzzle, but I did not know what it was.

While I tried to think of what it might be, my father began to walk across the room. "I can't believe it's you," he was saying. He reached toward my mother, walking slowly, as if in a dream. "I can't believe you're here. I thought you were gone." He pressed her to his chest.

"No, Paul," she said, twisting out from under his arms. "Paul," she said again, pushing him away. "There's someone you need to meet." She took the arm of the bee-voiced man in the thick red sweater. "This is Nathan," she said. She squeezed the man firmly, as if swearing a promise. "My husband."

The man looked uncomfortable. He made an *h*-sound, the beginning of "Hello," but cut himself short.

My father did not move, and I thought for a moment that he was going to fall over. He mouthed something under his breath. He stepped backward. I clung to his leg.

"And this," said my mother, pointing to the man in the blue uniform, "is Officer Hyatt. Four and a half years we've been looking for you, Paul."

It was not until much later that I learned the story of those years. This was the account that my mother told me, only once, when I was old enough to ask and she was not too old to answer. When she realized my father had taken me away from her, she had fallen into a great depression. Her recovery was slow, she said, and there were many things she did not remember about it, but when she regained herself, she was living in the care of her parents, who told her what the police had reported: that my father and I were very likely dead. "They're gone," her parents said. "You need to understand that, honey. No one's been able to find them." The police suggested she file the papers to have us declared deceased, but she would not. She returned to work, and met Nathan, and in time she married him, but she never accepted that I was lost to her.

She began her search for me shortly after my second birthday. She knew that my father had spoken of traveling north when it came time to flee the world, of taking refuge in the forests, and so she went to those places and hunted for us. She visited logging towns and trailer parks, dairy farms and lake resorts. She carried a photograph of the two of us, my round infant head held to my father's cheek, and she showed it to everyone she met. This man—she would say—the one in this picture, was crazy and had stolen her daughter. Have you seen him? Do you know his face? Can you help me find him? No, the people would answer. No, they hadn't. No, they couldn't. But eventually she met a man who recognized our faces. He had watched my father venture into the forest many times, he said, carrying tools and boxes and silver cans, and once he had even loaned him a shovel and a wheelbarrow, which my father had never returned. "I hope you find him," the man said. "That wheelbarrow cost me a pretty penny." And he shook his head and tucked a plug of tobacco into his mouth.

The woods in those parts were wild and rough, mostly untraveled, but once my mother knew we were there, it was only a matter of time before she was able to find us. She bought a topographic map from the state forestry commission, and she traced the lines of the streams on that map, and she journeyed along those streams into the forest. She came with her husband and the man in the blue uniform to take me into a new life, the life of her family, and away from the life that I knew—from the pantry full of cans and the dam with the broken turbine, from the cave with the frozen pool and the oak tree with the mossy hollow, from the way my father would carry me through the woods when I was tired, from the love that he showed me when I was unhappy, from the house and the bed and the world which were mine.

That afternoon, though, I knew none of these things.

"We need to go now," my mother said to me as I looked up at my father, who was blinking over and over again, staring into empty space. "Is there anything you want to take with you? Anything you need?" she asked. I shook my head, and when she reached down to touch me, I flinched. I understood nothing.

As we crossed the field that spread before our house, my father restrained by the man in the blue uniform, my mother walking beside me with her husband, I felt only a slight sense of dizziness, a weakness in my legs, as though my muscles and bones were coming loose from my body.

We traveled along the stream into the forest. My mother offered her help to me: "Are you doing okay? Can you make it past this puddle? Do you need me to lift you over? Here, take my hand."

But I did not listen.

I was watching the ground, and stirring the leaves, and holding tight to my father's hand, for no matter what they said to me, I would not let him go.

Acknowledgments

I owe thanks to my editor Jenny Minton, my agent Kyung Cho, the administrators of the James Michener–Paul Engle Fellowship for financial support, the friends and classmates who served as my first readers for these stories, and the long line of writing teachers who have helped me with my fiction: Judy Goss, Jan Donley, Michael Burns, Roland Sodowsky, Robert McLiam Wilson, Marilynne Robinson, James Alan McPherson, Judith Grossman, and Frank Conroy.

Permissions Acknowledgments

"These Hands" originally appeared in *The Georgia Review* and was published subsequently in *Prize Stories 1997: The O. Henry Awards* by Anchor Books, a division of Random House, Inc., New York, 1997. "Things That Fall from the Sky" originally appeared in *Crazyhorse.* "Apples" originally appeared in *The Chicago Tribune.* "A Day in the Life of Half of Rumpelstiltskin" originally appeared in *Writing on the Edge.* "The Ceiling" originally appeared in *McSweeney's.* "Space" originally appeared in *The Georgia Review.*

Grateful acknowledgment is made to the following for permission to reprint previously published material. Bug Music, Inc.: Excerpts from "Katie Belle Blue," written by Townes Van Zandt. Copyright © 1994 by Silver Dollar Music (ASCAP); Excerpt from "The Packard Company," written by William Morrisey. Copyright © 1991 by Dry Fly Music (BMI). Administered by BUG. All rights reserved. Reprinted by permission of Bug Music, Inc. Kevin Connolly, Inc.: Excerpt from "Goodnight" written by Kevin Connolly (www.kevinconnolly.com). Reprinted with permission of Kevin Connolly, Inc.